A PLACE CALLED PERFECT

A STORY BY HELENA DUGGAN

WhereverYouRoam Publishing

If you would like to talk to Boy or Violet please send them an email. They can't respond straight away as sometimes they're in school but they'll get back to you as soon as they can.

You can ask them any questions about their story but be careful, maybe only ask Boy about the Archers, talking about them scares Violet sometimes even though she says she's not a girly girl!

You'll find their contact details on helenaduggan.com

ISBN 978-1480093447

Typeset, Designed and Illustrated by Helena Duggan/Held Design
www.helddesign.ie

To Mam, the Original Dreamer.

CHAPTER 1

A Silent Protest

So what if this town wasn't perfect, who wanted perfect? Violet Brown flung herself onto her untidy bed. Polly, the most popular girl in school was perfect and BORING. Violet didn't want to be like Polly or be in a place that thought it was as perfect as Polly. How would she ever survive? She'd have to be neat and tidy; she'd definitely have to brush her hair and even probably clean her shoes. She'd have to be Polly.

"Never!" she roared loud enough for her parents to hear, then scrambled in under the safety of her duvet.

So what if her Dad was offered the best job an optician could ever get? He said 'it's a job amongst jobs'. It was probably like the Oscars of opticians, if the Oscars was a job and not an award for acting. His exact words were 'I'd be stupid, utterly stupid to turn it down'. This job meant so much to her Dad, other people's parents always talked about how much they hated their jobs. It was confusing, adults and jobs. Why did they work if they hated it? Violet hated maths and she never worked at that. They seemed to love holidays and always wanted to be somewhere else so why didn't they just do that? Why didn't they go on holidays forever, surely they'd be happy then. Adults loved to complain but not her Dad.

Eugene, that's what her Mam called him anytime he was in trouble, loved eyes. He just loved them. He said he married her Mam because she had the biggest eyes he'd ever seen, almost popped right out of her head sometimes. He loved being an optician. He left the house smiling every morning and always came home with a smile. He said because there were eyes everywhere he couldn't help himself. He loved blue eyes the best which was great because Violets eyes were blue, but he also liked brown ones and green ones came third. Everyday he thought up new ways to improve eyes. He'd even won an award and had just been on the cover of "Eye Spy" magazine. Her Mam said the whole world was talking about it, or at least the part of the world that loved eyes too. She said his new bosses read about it in "Eye Spy" and searched him out.

She was proud of her Dad. She loved him more than a billion pounds. She was happy for him too, but being happy for him didn't mean she was happy. She didn't want the same things as her Dad. Her Mam would follow him 'to the ends of the world' as they were 'hopelessly in love'. They said that so many times it made Violet cringe, other people's parents didn't talk like that.

But that was the thing with parents, they only ever did what they wanted and kids had to obey. Sometimes she wished she had brothers and sisters, then there'd be more on her side. She didn't want the best job in the world, she just wanted to spend the rest of the summer playing up the fields with her friends. She'd barely have anytime to say goodbye either. Her Dad said they wanted him to start 'asap', that meant 'really quickly' because they were leaving on Sunday. Her Dad would start work Monday morning.

The town was called "Perfect". She laughed. How could she ever live in a place called Perfect?. It couldn't be perfect anyway, there had to be something wrong with it. Violet pulled back the duvet and walked to the window. She sat there in the fading evening light and well into the night plotting a way out of her problem. The more she thought the more her head hurt and she still hadn't come up with a proper plan. She could run away but she was only ten and would need her parents for at least another two years, maybe three to be safe. She decided she'd sleep on the problem.

The next morning she woke with a smile. She had it. She wasn't going to talk to her Dad at all, not just for a day or two, this plan was much bigger than that. She wouldn't talk to him for as long as it took to change his mind. It was going to be hard but if she concentrated she could do it.

After all it was her Dad who told her she could be whatever she wanted to be. So that was the plan, she was going to be silent.

CHAPTER 2

Tea For Three

Sunday came too quickly, probably because they'd spent all day Saturday packing. When she wanted time to go slowly, it always went fast, so all day Saturday Violet begged for time to go fast, her mother called it 'reverse scientology', but it didn't work, before she knew it, she'd cried her goodbyes and was in the back of the car on the way to Perfect.

"Where is this place Mam?" she asked, slotting her head between the two front seats.

"Ask your father pet, he knows more than me," her mother smiled.

Violet sat back in her spot and let silence flood the car.

"Are you still not talking to me?" her Dad said, after a while.

She didn't reply. She hated not talking to him.

"Well we're not too far now pet," he sighed.

He looked at his wife who gently squeezed his hand. Violet cringed, slumped down in her seat and closed her eyes.

She woke with a jerk, as the car crunched to a stop over squashed gravel. It was dark. She pulled herself up from the warm leather seat and peered out the back window. She gasped and ducked back down. Two dark figures, one tall, one small, stood shadowed in the light from the house door. Violet's father looked at her mother then unbuckled his seat belt and stepped out of the car.

"Ah Mr. and Mr. Archer," her father said, approaching the strangers, "we didn't expect a welcoming commitee."

"Well of course Mr. Brown, we wanted to see you settled," the tall man said, extending his hand.

"We've been preparing all day. The house is spick and span and we've the kettle on the boil," the small man said, stepping in front of the larger one to grab her father's hand, "Leave your stuff in the car and come in for a brew. I'm sure you must all be exhausted."

"Of course, how kind," her mother said, reaching the front door to greet both men, "we'd love a cuppa. Great idea."

The four entered the house leaving Violet to fume in her seat, forgotten again.

"Violet come in from the car pet, it's freezing out there," her father's voice called from across the gravel yard.

She smiled, he didn't forget. She pushed open the heavy car door and poked her head out to look left and right. The driveway was dark and surrounded by large trees. Huge twisted branches cast ghostly shadows over the gravel. She shivered. Suddenly the wind whistled through the yard and the leaves began to whisper. Violet jumped back and slammed the door, locking herself safely inside the car. She'd have to run for it, she took a deep breath. On the count of three.

"One, two, threeeee..."

She flung open the car door, jumped and ran, not looking left or right at the creatures who watched from the darkness. She raced for the house, bounded up the steps and jumped over the threshold. Just as she slammed the door, she heard laughter echo through the trees. She slid down the wall, onto the hall floor trying to catch her breath. Surely it wasn't laughter, it must have been the wind.

"Violet is that you pet?" her mother called, from down the hallway, "come in and say hello to our guests."

Putting the laughter to the back of her mind, she pushed up from the floor, pulled off her shoes and threw them by the door. The hall was covered in shiny, cream tiles perfect for socks. She took a run and slid the whole way into the room straight ahead, coming to a rest by the kitchen table. Four pairs of eyes stared at her, two in embarrassment, two in shock.

"Violet!" her father snapped, "we have guests."

She didn't respond. Quickly her father covered the silence introducing her to the strange men that sat round the table.

"Violet this is Mr. George Archer."

"Just George is fine," the tall man said, standing up from the table to shake her hand.

She tried not to laugh. George Archer was so tall he couldn't stand straight in the room. His head bent to one side almost touching his shoulder. Everything about him was long, from his spindly arms and legs to his pencil thin nose that almost divided his face in two. His head was completely bald and creamy white like a chocolate egg. Clearly uncomfortable, he quickly sat back down.

"And I'm Edward, you must be Violet?" the smaller of the Archers said, as he stood to shake her hand.

Again she had to stop herself laughing. She was the same height as him and Violet wasn't even the tallest in her class. Mr. Edward Archer was very small for his age. Though small, he was very wide and square, as though he were made from blocks. His head was square, his nose was square and squished. His eyes, the only part of his body that wasn't square, stuck out a little, like they were trying to escape from his face.

The two brothers wore the same brown suits and shiny brown shoes. Edward Archer wore a funny brown bowler hat just like the one on her mother's favourite painting of a man with no face. Mr. George Archer didn't wear a hat but that was probably because it would fall off everytime he stood up inside.

Both of them had redish eyes hidden behind round gold framed glasses, it looked a little scary until George Archer took his off.

> "Oh it's the glass!" Violet smiled at the taller twin, "Why is the glass red?"

George Archer pushed his glasses back onto his nose and scowled.

> "Well Violet dear," Edward Archer said, "It's a funny story really and one we hope your father will help us to solve. You see this town is perfect except for one curious fact. Every single inhabitant here wears glasses. We've had numerous scientists look at our situation.

They say it's because we're so close to the sun. You and your family Violet will find after only a short length of time in Perfect, your eyesight will get dusty, the edges of your vision will blur and eventually you will go blind."

"Mam!" she shouted, trying not to cry, "I don't want to go blind. I like being able to see. I knew we shouldn't have moved here."

"Oh no," Edward Archer laughed, "I certainly didn't mean to frighten you Violet dear. I assure you the effects are only temporary, once one has left this town of ours they wear off. Also, we have found a clever way around our little problem," he said pointing to his glasses, "These work a treat. You'll find everybody is wearing them. Quite in vogue as they say."

"You'll have to visit our spectacle shop dear so we can fit you a pair," George Archer smiled.

Violet grabbed her mother's skirt.

"I don't want to wear glasses Mam, there's nothing wrong with my eyes."

"I know Violet," her mother shushed, looking anxiously at her husband, "but it's only for a short time. Your father will fix the problem."

"Don't worry Violet," her Dad said, bending down to pick her up.

She moved round her mother's back away from his arms.

"She's tired," he sighed, his cheeks a little red, "I think it's time for bed."

"Oh no, not yet," George Archer said quickly, "you must have some tea. It's a tradition here."

"Oh yes," Edward Archer smiled, grabbing cups from the worktop, "It's custom I assure you."

"I don't like tea," Violet said, looking at her mother.

"You'll like this one," George Archer smiled.

Violet didn't like the Archers, there was something scary about them but if she didn't have the tea she'd be killed and she was in enough trouble already. Her parents looked at each other as they sat down at the table. They seemed happy to drink it and they weren't stupid Violet hoped. She sat down between her father and mother. Edward Archer sat on the other side waiting for his brother to finish pouring.

"This tea is a speciality of Perfect. You'll find most people drink at least a cup a day. It's a tea mad town," Edward said when all the cups were filled,

"Now imagine the nicest taste you can think of then take a sip."

Violet did as she was told. She imagined her father's favourite drink, which was hers too, ice cream sundae he called it. Big bits of cold vanilla ice cream dunked in fizzy orange. She saw the froth-like clouds bubbling over the top of the glass and tasted the burst of flavour as it hit her tongue. She was almost licking her lips as she raised her mug of tea. The vanilla tingled her nose. She tipped the mug to take a sip, careful not to burn her lips. The tea bubbled and fizzed as she gulped the mixture of vanilla and orange heaven. She couldn't believe it. She opened her eyes to make sure no one had swapped her cup. The light brown coloured tea smiled back at her. She looked at her mother and father, their eyes were still shut and silly smiles sat on their faces.

"I think I'll have another cup," her father said a little later, reaching for the steaming pot.

"We thought you might," both Archers replied in unison.

They sat round the table and finished the pot while the Archers filled them in on their new home.

Later that night, Violet climbed beneath her new sheets in her new room. The town seemed nice enough from what the

Archer's had said but she'd made up her mind, she didn't and wouldn't like it. She turned off the lights and slipped into a perfect nights sleep.

.

CHAPTER 3

The Spectacle Makers Shop

The morning sun warmed Violet's face and gently pulled her from her dreams. She'd slept like a log in her new bed.

She'd stretched and sat up before she realised something was wrong. She could faintly see the edges of her room but everything straight in front of her was covered by a big black blob, like ink had leaked all over her eyes. She rubbed them but nothing changed, she still couldn't see. Her heart beat a little faster. She stuck her foot out of the duvet and stretched for the floor

"Ouch," she yelled, smacking her toe off something solid as she walked blindly towards the door.

"Mam, Dad!" she cried.

"Violet, Violet, what is it?" croaked her Dad's sleepy voice.

Suddenly a crash shook the house.

"Eugene!" her mother cried, "Eugene what's happened, are you okay?"

Violet gingerly felt her way out the door and down the hall to her parent's room.

"Mam, Dad, I can't see!" she stumbled inside.

"Neither can I pet," her father replied, his voice cheerful, "It's nothing to panic about, we were warned."

"But not this soon Eugene!" her mother shouted.

"No need to panic girls," he repeated, his voice now a little high pitched.

"Violet come over and get into bed with your mother. I'll go downstairs and see if I can get a hold of the Archers. They'll know what to do."

"But how Eugene, you can't see either?" her mother sobbed.

"Don't worry about me," he replied, tripping over Violet who was now crawling across the carpet.

"Oh what a good idea pet!" he said, easing gently onto his knees, "Now I'll be back soon with help, trust me."

Violet heard her father crawl baby like across the room and out into the hall. She didn't want to trust him. He didn't deserve her trust. This was all his fault.

"Ow," she cried, banging into the side of her parent's bed.

"You okay pet?" her mother called from above.

Violet rubbed her forehead searching for blood but felt nothing watery.

"Ya I think so," she said, crawling in beside her Mam.

The mattress on her side was still warm and smelt like her dad, it made her angry.

"Good morning!" a voice called from outside her parent's window, "it's a glorious day family Brown."

"Mam, there's someone outside."

"I know pet, stay here," her mother whispered, then disappeared from her spot.

Violet heard her stumble across the room, then the window squeaked and cold air tickled her toes. She pulled them up and wrapped the duvet tighter to block all air holes.

"Hello?" her mother called.

"Oh good morning Mrs. Brown, I just stopped by to see

how your first day is going and to offer Eugene a lift to work."

"Oh Mr. Archer," her mother gasped, "what a god send you are. I'm afraid we have all woken up a little worse for wear. The effects of the sun have come on sooner than expected."

"Oh no," Mr. Archer replied, "that's a pity. You won't get to see our beautiful town through your naked eyes. Oh well, sometimes it happens that way. Not to worry stay put and I will take it from here. We'll have you back to normal in no time."

In a few minutes Mr. Edward Archer, Violet knew it was him because he was the same height as her, had led them from the room into the back of his car.

"Now onto our spectacle makers emporium," he called, as the engine whistled into life.

Violet always thought a spectacle was when she was doing something wrong, her mother regularly told her 'to stop making a spectacle of herself', now she knew it meant glasses. Emporium was more difficult but she had a feeling it was a posh word for shop. The Archers seemed to like posh words.

As Mr. Edward Archer led her by the arm slowly down the

stone path towards his shop, Violet decided she never wanted to be blind again. She liked her sight, already she really missed colour, everything in her new world was black and fuzzy. She wished for some orange or purple or even some grey though that wasn't really a colour.

"Mind the steps now Violet," Mr. Edward Archer said.

Suddenly the black got blacker and she stumbled backwards.

"Oh don't worry Violet dear, we're just coming inside, the light will change a little," Edward Archer laughed.

Violet smiled to be polite but inside she was fuming, she was blind and he was laughing. She'd half decided already but his laugh made it a fact, she hated Edward Archer.

"Now I'm just going to lower you into this chair," he said, grabbing her hands.

Violet did as she was told and winced as the cold leather touched her bare legs, she was still wearing her short pyjamas, the furry love hearted pair. She blushed as she pictured the pink and red pattern. She'd told her mam she was getting too old for love hearts but parents never listened.

"I'm just going to get your mother and father dear," Edward Archer called, his footsteps fading into the distance.

Silence filled the shop.

A lot of the time Violet liked silence, but not this time. Blindness turned silence scary. She pushed her hands in under her thighs, swung her legs and tried to remember a happy song.

Something rustled nearby. She turned quickly. Suddenly someone blew in her ear and laughed. It was the same laugh, the one she had heard the night before.

She gasped, "Who's there?"

"Hey you!" a voice shouted.

Her chair was knocked sideways and she hit her head. Footsteps raced through the shop and glass smashed behind her.

"Who's there?" she cried, grabbing the chair arms.

"Violet dear, what are you doing here?"

It was a voice she recognised.

"There was somebody here, there was a fight."

"Really?" Mr. George Archer replied sounding worried, "Did you see them dear? What did they look like?"

"No," Violet said quickly, "I'm blind but I heard them. One of them blew in my ear!"

"Ah," George Archer laughed, "Losing ones sight can play havoc with ones hearing."

"No there really was someone here, I swear," Violet protested.

"No there wasn't Violet," George Archer snapped.

She was about to argue when she heard her parents shuffle into the room.

"Mam, Dad is that you?" she said leaning out of her chair.

Someone grabbed her shoulders and pulled her back.

"Lots of glass to be broken here Violet," George Archer snarled.

"Violet don't worry we're here pet," her Dad soothed, he sounded nearby.

She wanted to reply but couldn't, she was still angry with him.

"Now you're first Violet," Edward Archer said, "I do hope these fit. If not we can adjust them, you have a rather large head for someone so young."

Violet winced as glasses were shoved onto the bridge of her nose. Then hands cupped either side of her face and adjusted the frames.

"Now," Edward Archer said, "Open your eyes dear and tell us what you see."

Violet held her breath afraid she might still be blind and slowly opened her eyes. She gasped as colour filled her vision. Rich browns from the dark wood that panelled the shop walls, deep red from the luxurious carpet at her feet and bright gold from the spectacles resting inside sparkling glass cabinets. It was the poshest place she'd ever seen.

"Is there something wrong?" Edward Archer asked.

"No," Violet stammered, "it's just I've never been in a place like this before, it's amazing!"

Pride passed between the brothers.

"We try our best," Edward replied.

As the Archers moved onto her parents, Violet took her chance to explore.

Everything in the shop was shiny, even the gold handles on the cabinet doors shone. The room she was in was at least her Dad and a half high and glass cabinets filled the shop from floor to ceiling. A huge wooden ladder on wheels rested against one of the walls and George Archer was just stepping off it with a pair of specs in hand.

"For your mother," he smiled pushing past.

Violet moved away from her parents, slipping in round the back of the chair she'd been sitting on. A thin thread of light leaked through a gap in the wood panel in front of her. Gently she pushed on the wall and it gave way revealing an entrance into a room behind.

This room was stacked floor to ceiling with books. The books were old, their worn covers battered and bruised. They were the type of dusty books her mother hated but her father loved. She pulled one out, *An Optical Illusion*, then another *Blind Mans Bluff* and another *Seeing Things*. She scanned the shelves and noticed all the books were the same, they were all about eyes. She was going to pick up another when she heard a voice.

"Don't even think about it."

She turned quickly and looked straight into the face of Mr. George Archer who was on his knees.

"Perfect kids must act perfectly!" he scowled.

Violet froze.

"There you are George," Edward Archer said, peeping through the door, "I see you found Violet. We were worried dear."

Saved by the interruption, Violet raced past Edward Archer to the safety of her parents.

There was something different about the Archers as Violet studied them from behind her mother's chair. Edward the smaller of the two somehow wasn't so small and his head not so large. His eyes weren't bulging and his teeth were somehow straighter. George too had changed, he didn't look so tall, his eyes fitted his face and his arms and legs weren't so spindly. He even stood tall without bending his head which was very strange. The changes were small but added together they meant the Archers weren't as ugly as Violet remembered. You might even say they looked nice. It didn't mean she was starting to like them; there was still something strange about the pair, she just couldn't put her finger on it.

She looked at her parents who now both wore glasses. Her mother was lovely even with the frames but she had always been beautiful and Violet hoped someday she'd be compared to her mother. Her father too looked handsome, he even had more hair. They were the perfect couple and Violet couldn't believe she hadn't noticed it before.

"Violet," her mother said, "those glasses really suit you. You look beautiful!"

She returned her mother's smile, Perfect was sending them all a little mushy. She was even thinking about giving the place a chance, fighting it just felt like hard work. For today, just for today, she'd give in to Perfect.

CHAPTER 4

First Sons of Perfect

The Archers, because of what happened, gave her Dad the day off. So, after a quick visit home to change out of their pyjamas, it was decided the family would head into the town and have a look around.

The best way to see Perfect was on foot Edward Archer said. So they left their house and followed the directions into town. Violet couldn't believe how quickly she'd gotten used to wearing her glasses as if they'd been stuck on her face forever. Everything was crystal clear and, she had to admit, kinda nice.

The road into town was tree lined. The trees were exactly the same distance apart, Violet measured them by counting her footsteps. Every sixty steps there was a tree, except when there was a bench, which happened every one hundred and eighty steps or three trees apart. The sun was shining and the sky, a bright blue, was filled with candyfloss clouds. Everything was neat and tidy. Wild flowers grew in neat bunches and there wasn't bird poo anywhere though the trees were full of birds. They probably had their own toilet Violet laughed running ahead of her parents. As the family turned a corner about half a mile from their house, the town came into view. Violet stopped.

It was like something from a fairytale. The streets were narrow and cobbled just like the path that led to the Archers shop. The buildings were white and wooden beams ran this way and that across their fronts. They were all sorts of shapes and sizes, some tall and narrow, some squatty and broad. Each one leaned over a little, sheltering the roadways below. It made Perfect look cosy. The town was the prettiest Violet had ever seen. She was afraid she was starting to like the place.

Everybody they passed in the town smiled at the new arrivals as if they were locals. Some even greeted them by name.

> "It's a small town dear, something we'll have to get used to," her father said, when her mother questioned the friendliness of the locals.

> "Oh I think I'm used to it already Eugene. This place feels like home, it's what we've been searching for. I'm so glad you brought us here."

What? Her now gushing mother had hated the thoughts of the move. She'd said loads of times that she was only doing it for the sake of her husband. Her change of heart was quick.

"I think I could live here forever," her mother smiled, grabbing her husband's hand.

Her Dad beamed and kissed his wife's forehead.

"What about you Violet?" he asked.

"It's alright."

She didn't want to give in, even answering her Dad was a big step. She'd leave the gooey stuff to her mother. Anyway she hadn't made up her mind about Perfect yet.

As they walked through the town she began to notice some strange things. The streets were perfectly clean. She hadn't seen any rubbish, not even a sweet wrapper but there were no bins anywhere. The people were all skinny, there wasn't a fat one in sight and though they all looked different there was something similar about all of them. It was like a gloss or shine, somehow everyone glowed.

"They're healthy Violet," her father said, "The Archers told me this is rated as the healthiest town in all the world."

Violet believed him, she hadn't spotted a chippers anywhere and she loved fish and chips on a Sunday evening. She noted that down as another black mark against the town.

As her parents were busy chatting she quietly slipped off the main road down one of the side alleys. She was dying to explore. Normally side roads were dirty and dark and she would never go down one alone but this town was different. She wasn't scared at all as she walked the spotless alley.

A plaque mounted on the wall of one of the houses caught her eye and she stopped to read it.

> *Behold The Birth Place of Messrs George, Edward and William Archer, first sons of Perfect.*

It must be the Archers she knew, but she'd never heard of William. She moved closer for a look. Something about the house was not right. A hanging basket over the entrance was crooked and the faded blue paint on the door, worn and chipped. She peered through the murky glass window trying to ignore her mother's warning voice in her head, 'mind your own business Violet!' She wouldn't normally stare into someone else's home, but by Perfect's standards this house was derelict. Her nose had just touched the glass when a ghostly face zoomed forward from the darkness inside. She squealed, jumping back.

An old woman stared out through the dirt. Skin sagged from her bones and whispy white hair fell from her balding scalp. Her mouth was gapped in blackened teeth.

Violet tripped over a loose lace knocking off her glasses as she raced from the window. She fumbled onto her knees to search the cobblestone when laughter filled the laneway. The same laughter had followed her since her family's arrival. She found the frames, shoved them quickly on, scrambled up and sprinted away from the house, not daring to look back.

CHAPTER 5

Dreams of Ghostly Boys

After only two weeks in the new town, Summer was over. Violet didn't like starting a new school or making new friends. She had tried to make some already but it didn't work. She wasn't like them, she didn't have the shine every Perfect person had. The kids in the town were nice. They talked to her and some even asked if she wanted to play. That was it though, they were too nice.

Her mother wouldn't listen.

> "I'm sick of it Violet, too nice, what does that mean? You'll really have to start making an effort here. You're embarrassing me in front of all the other mums!"

'Mums', when did her Mam ever use a word like 'Mums'?

Violet's Mam was never like her friends mothers. She didn't bake, burnt every dinner she ever made and always wore odd socks. But in this town she was different.

Everyday she got up early and made breakfast for the family.

Once she'd said goodbye to Violet's Dad and cleaned the house, she'd head out to meet her new friends, the ones whose children Violet had to pretend to like. Sometimes it was for bookclub, or cookery lessons or even golf. In her short time in Perfect Violet's mam had become head of the town's baking committee. Her mother was delighted, she smiled from ear to ear when she got the phonecall and baked cupcakes for the rest of the night. The cupcakes were nice but it was still a little odd. Her old mother was a terrible cook, hated golf and would laugh at the idea of bookclub. Now she was a "Perfectionist" and shone like everyone else.

Her Dad had changed too but his change was different. He wasn't shiny at all. He was dull, lifeless and always tired. Even his smile had faded. He looked older, in two weeks he'd put on five years. Violet had never seen him sad and felt partly to blame. She still wasn't speaking to him. They used to talk about everything, but for the last twelve days and five hours she hadn't said a word. In the beginning he tried to talk but by day four he'd given up too.

The way her parents were around each other was also different. Before they were never apart, always hugging and kissing which was really embarrassing. Now Violet wanted to be embarrassed even just for a second. Her mother acted perfect and her Dad, who began to look like a homeless person, worked forever locked in his office. They didn't talk like they used to.

The night before school started Violet overheard her parents in the kitchen as she climbed the stairs to bed. Her father's voice made her stop. He sounded worried.

"Rose," he sighed, "will you please put that away and sit down. I need to speak to you."

"Have a word from there," her mother replied, "I'm almost finished this pastry. I can hear you perfectly from here."

"Rose. Please. Now," her father almost shouted.

Violet stiffened. She'd never heard her father that angry before.

"Just a minute darling, I'm almost finished."

"I thought you hated cooking?" he snapped.

"Oh no, what ever made you think that? I love it. Since I've moved here a whole new world has opened up."

"I'm worried about this place," his voice softened.

What was that darling?"

A chair scraped the kitchen tiles then heavy footsteps headed across the kitchen. Violet froze.

"Rose," he father said, stopping in the doorway.

"Yes darling?"

"You know I love you, don't you?" he sounded lonely.

"Of course darling. Now do you want sprinkles on your buns or will I make icing? The ladies loved the icing last time round."

Her father didn't reply. He left the kitchen and headed up the hall. As quietly as Violet could she climbed the stairs and jumped in under her duvet. A few minutes later her Dad's figure appeared in the doorway.

"Violet," he whispered, "are you awake?"

She pulled the covers tight, rolled over and pretended to sleep. Her father tiptoed across the floorboards and sat gently onto the edge of her bed. Violet's heart beat faster. He rubbed her hair. She wanted to sit up and hug him, she knew he was sad but she couldn't. He had gotten them into this mess.

"Violet," he whispered, his voice was shaky, "I love you pet."

He bent down and kissed her forehead, gently tucked in the edges of the blankets and slipped quietly from the room. She opened her eyes. What had gotten into her family?

Her parents were crazy. It made her sad to see her Dad so upset but in another way it made her happy. He wasn't enjoying their new home and the more he didn't like it, the quicker they would move.

Violet stayed awake for a long time. She was nervous about school the next day and couldn't sleep. At about four in the morning footsteps passed her door heading downstairs. It was her Dad, his shadow outlined by the dim morning light. She began to doze off listening for his return when something hit the floor.

Quickly she reached for her glasses on the bedside table. She ran her hand blindly across the smooth wood but found nothing. She threw her arm over the side of the bed and felt along the floor.

"You're new here, aren't ya?"

Violet jumped and ducked back in under the blankets. Someone laughed. It was that laugh again.

"Why are you hiding? Sure you can't see me anyway ya eejit!"

Violet pulled the duvet down a little to peer. The room was fuzzy but she could make out a black shadow moving in the corner. Quickly she ducked back under.

"What do you want?" she shouted, her voice muffled by the sheets.

"I want all your money and as many penny sweets as you can get or the doll gets it!"

"I don't know where to get penny sweets" Violet quivered.

The boy laughed again. She was sure it was a boy.

"I'm only messing, you really are some eejit! Oh no," he sounded panicked, "I have to go they're coming. Here're your glasses. Enjoy school tomorrow!"

Something landed on the covers and she reached out to find her glasses. Footsteps ran through the room as if three or four people were fighting at the end of her bed. Quickly she pushed on her frames. Everything stopped.

She turned on the bedside lamp. The room was empty. Her heart pounded as she pulled the blankets back over her head. She fell asleep a little later, her dreams full of ghostly boys.

CHAPTER 6

School Rules

Violet got up early the next morning after a restless night hidden under her sheets and went downstairs to have breakfast. She walked into the kitchen where her father was half asleep over some papers at the table. He quickly sat up and gathered in his notes.

"You're up early pet," he said, almost knocking over a cold cup of tea.

"I couldn't sleep," she replied, the words were brief but it was a relief to say something after such a long silence.

"Me either."

Her Dad smiled warmly trying to hide his surprise.

"What ya doing?" Violet asked.

"Just research for work," he said, packing the pages away under his notepad.

"Is it for the Archers?"

He nodded and pushed his chair back from the table.

"Would you like some cereal pet?"

"Dad," Violet said, "do you like the Archers?"

"Of course pet. They're my bosses."

"It's just well there's something strange about them and this place. Don't you think Mam is being a bit weird?"

"Violet, don't say something like that about your mother. It's just the stress of the move. You've been hard on this place since we got here. Give it a chance!" he suddenly snapped.

For the second time in not even a day there was anger in his voice. What was it with adults, last night he sounded like he wasn't sure about the town either.

"I hate it here Dad, I hate this place, I never wanted to move here. You made us and now everything is gone strange even Mam and you!" Violet roared, storming from the room.

"Violet get back here this minute!"

His tone was terrifying and even though she wanted to be brave and walk away, she turned around and edged back into the doorway.

"Don't you ever speak to me like that again. I am trying to make a life for us here. I know it's difficult, it is not easy to move at your age but you have to give this place a chance."

"At my age! I'm ten Dad, I'm not a baby. I have given this place a chance but I hate it, I HATE it Dad. Even last night I couldn't sleep because there was someone in my room. I wasn't even going to tell you because I knew you wouldn't believe me."

"What do you mean someone in your room?"

"I heard voices Dad. It was a boy, he talked to me!"

"Violet it's just your imagination. It's a new house. Look pet we're all trying to find our feet here. You'll make lots of new friends today and you'll forget we ever had this fight."

"No I won't Dad. You never listen to me. I wish I never started talking to you again!" she screamed and ran from the kitchen.

This time she didn't turn back though her Dad called her name. She sprinted up the stairs, slammed her door and flung herself onto the bed. For a while her Dad banged around in the kitchen below, then the front door clattered, the car roared to life and he was gone.

Violet cried into her pink cotton sheets loud enough so her mother would hear. She wanted her Mam to give her a hug and whisper that everything would be okay. First her Mam changed, then her Dad. Now Violet had nobody. She was alone. Her Mam never came and she got ready for her first day of school by herself.

"Were you fighting with your father this morning Violet?" her mother asked when she joined her in the kitchen.

"No," Violet answered, her voice teary.

"Are you okay pet?"

She raised her red rimmed eyes to meet her mother's.

"I'm fine."

"Oh good," her mother smiled, "I've made you ham sandwiches for lunch and a bun. Now brush your hair Violet, don't want you looking a mess in front of all the other mothers."

They walked in silence to school. The playground was full when they got there and some of the kids waved at Violet as she passed through on the way to the principal's office. After a quick introduction she said goodbye to her mother and followed the principal to her classroom.

She stood nervously at the front of the class as the principal whispered something to her new teacher. In her old school the minute teacher was distracted, they would talk, pass notes and sometimes even switch seats. Here it was different, the students sat in silence. They didn't even smile.

The teacher Mrs. Moody was short, round and granny old. She wore the usual glasses, a blue skirt, red cardigan and a white shirt. She had the shine.

> "Violet dear," she said as the principal left the room, "take a seat. There is one free at the back."

Violet walked to the end of the room and took a seat between a girl with pigtails and a curly haired boy. They both smiled as she sat down.

> "Now class, say hello to Violet."

Like a choir everyone responded, giving Violet the loudest "Hello" she'd ever heard. Then the teacher got her to stand up and tell the class about her life before Perfect. Every student listened. No one chewed a pencil, chatted, fidgeted or did anything normal. When she'd finished talking about herself, teacher gave the class some work and came down to Violet.

> "Violet dear," she whispered, "We have a few tests here that each new student has to take. It's so we can tell where you fit."

"What do you mean?" Violet asked.

She didn't fit in anywhere.

"It's nothing to worry about. We just like to assess all our students. To tell what standard you are at and if you have any defaults, I mean problems we should be aware of."

"Oh no teacher, I don't have any problems," Violet smiled as nicely as possible.

"I don't mean problems as such dear. It's just in this school we have a certain student we nurture, the perfect student. Not all our pupils are perfect when they come to us. Take Michael over there," the teacher said, pointing to a blonde haired boy busy doing his maths problem, "he was quite excitable when he came to us, couldn't sit still for a minute but we soon worked that out of him and now he's picture perfect."

"Oh I can sit still," Violet insisted, disliking her new teacher's tone.

"I'm sure you can Violet dear but there are all sorts of afflictions students are burdened with. We have had some here that made up stories, some that doodled all day, others like Michael that couldn't sit still. The list goes on. I am sure you are not burdened with any such problems dear but we do need to know. Now it won't take long."

Swiftly Mrs. Moody put a piece of paper onto Violet's desk and held a pencil out in front of her. Violet looked at the pencil then back at her teacher who nodded towards the object in her hand.

"Take it dear," she smiled.

Violet reached up and took the pencil.

"Ah left handed. Thought as much," the teacher tutted as she walked away.

Confused, Violet looked down at the paper on her desk. Question one: What is your name? She tried not to laugh as she filled in the empty box. The questions got stranger. Have you ever had an imaginary friend? Do you ever day dream? Have you ever felt the urge to run away from home? Do you question adults? She didn't know what to write and had only filled in a few lines by lunch time.

She followed an orderly line out of the classroom and into the concrete playground. The sun was shining but everything looked grey. There was no life in the yard, no screaming, shouting or laughing which was normal in her old school.

Nobody ran, there was no football, no tig, nothing. She tried not to think about her old friends and what they were doing right now as she sat down on a bench by the wall.

"Hello Violet."

She looked up from her lunch. It was a red haired girl she recognised from class.

"I'm Beatrice. Would like to join us for a game of skip?"

"Oh em...yeah I'd love to," Violet replied.

Beatrice smiled and Violet walked with her new friend over to a group of girls standing around a long skipping rope.

"Who'd like to hold first?" Beatrice asked.

Violet stepped forward but the red haired girl held up her hand.

"Not straight away Violet. You have to learn how to swing the rope first."

Violet blushed and stepped back into the comfort of the crowd. She didn't know there were skipping rules. When the game started, each girl stepped into the rope and jumped exactly three times. There was no laughing or joking and the game was held to strict rules. When it came to Violet's turn she jumped nervously in, the first two skips were great and she relaxed.

To liven the group, she decided to try a trick she'd practised at home for her third skip. The rope came round and she crossed her legs as it passed beneath her. Immediately the skipping stopped and everybody turned towards her.

"That's not in the rules," Beatrice barked.

"I'm sorry," Violet stuttered.

"It's not in the rules Violet," Beatrice repeated again, "If it is not in the rules then you can't do it. What do you think rules are for?!"

Violet didn't know what to say as she looked around at the disgusted faces. Suddenly Beatrice began to swing the rope once more.

"It's okay Violet," she smiled as though nothing had happened, "maybe you should sit this round out to watch."

She did what she was told, found a spot a little back from the game and watched. The girls jumped like robots until the bell rang. Immediately everything stopped and the pupils filed back into their classrooms. Violet had never seen anything like it.

This town definitely wasn't perfect for children. Back inside she started filling out the rest of the strange questionnaire. Why would the school need to know her first pet's name and if she visited her grandmother a lot. She was just writing that she didn't have a grandmother when the pencil slipped from her hand onto the wooden floor. It was out of reach so she slipped off her seat in under the desk. As she stretched for the pencil she noticed something etched into the bottom of her desk.

William Archer was here, full of life and nothing to fear. 1965

She turned awkwardly in the small space and ran her fingers over the roughly scrawled words. It was that name again, William Archer. Weird that the Archers or her parents never mentioned William. He was definitely the coolest brother. Edward or George would never scratch their names into a desk, no one in the town would. No wonder William left. She crawled back out and took her seat. Just as she was about to start writing again, she sensed the silence and looked up. For the second time that day all eyes were on her.

"You've decided to rejoin us I see," Mrs. Moody smiled.

"Oh I em... I dropped my pencil," she said, holding it up.

"And you didn't think to ask permission?"

"Oh I em..."

Permission to pick up a pencil sounded silly.

"Rules Violet," the teacher snapped, "Beatrice told me about the skipping incident and now this. I'm afraid I will have to call your parents."

Her parents called for a skipping trick and a lost pencil!

"But...I just..."

"No buts Violet. You are on thin ice as it is my dear. Now class back to work." Mrs. Moody smiled.

Violet sat shocked for a while before resuming her questions. She had to get out of Perfect. Angrily she scribbled down the colour of her favourite pair of socks. William Archer must have gotten away and if he could do it she could too, parents or no parents.

CHAPTER 7

IDDCS

The following evening Violet was at the kitchen table doing her homework when her mother walked in.

"I've been speaking to your teacher Violet," she sighed, sitting down, "You've been acting up in class, she said you are not integrating with the other students..."

She left the sentence hang for a moment. Violet tried to speak but her mother held up a hand.

"They analysed your test results. I can't believe I never saw it before. It's my fault. I take full responsibility."

"What do you mean Mam? What test?"

"Violet please, I know it's just your condition talking but don't answer back to your mother."

"Mam," Violet pleaded, "If you are talking about that test yesterday it was the stupidest thing I have ever seen. They even asked me the colour of my favourite pair of socks. You would have laughed. It's strange here Mam, I don't like this place..."

"Stop it Violet, I won't hear another word said. You know colour can tell a lot about a person, especially the colour of their socks! Now Violet dear..." she continued.

Her mother had never called her "dear" before. She sounded like Mrs. Moody.

"You have a condition called IDDCS. It's Irritable, Disfunctional, Disobedient Child Syndrome. I can't believe I never picked up on it before. It has probably afflicted you all your life pet," she said, reaching into her pocket, "we're putting you on these."

She pulled out a small brown bottle and placed it on the table in front of Violet.

"You'll take one of these in the morning," she said, shaking a blue pill out onto her hand.

Then her mother got up, filled a glass with water and left it and the pill down in front of her daughter.

"And two of these in the evening," she said, reaching into her other pocket to pull out a bottle of yellow pills.

"And don't worry about remembering dear. Mrs. Moody

kindly gave me this alarm so I can set a reminder," she said, placing a strange looking clock in the centre of the table, "They really do look out for your wellbeing in that school. I don't know what we'd do without them."

"But Mam, I've only been there a day. Mrs. Moody doesn't even know me. The test was stupid and I wasn't disobedient! I dropped my pencil and crossed my legs in skipping. Mam please, I don't want to take pills. There is nothing wrong with me!"

"Violet, stop it now! I know it's your condition talking but I do find it hard to take sometimes."

"Mam," Violet persisted.

"Enough dear! Swallow that now. I have to meet my bookclub this evening and I don't want to worry that you haven't taken your pills."

Violet glanced down at the blue pill then back at her mother who looked like she was going to explode. She picked it up, placed it on her tongue, took a gulp of water and swallowed. Her mother smiled, patted her daughter's head and rose from the table.

"Now I bet you feel better already. I'm going out but

I will be back in time to get you and your father's tea. Risotto tonight I think."

Her mother floated from the room leaving Violet angry at the kitchen table. The woman she just talked to, though she looked like her mother, was definitely not her mother. She had to be an imposter. Violet got up from the table and paced the room. Something had to be done. She had to try to get through to her father one last time. He was at work so she grabbed her coat and ran as fast as her legs could carry her all the way to the Archers shop.

CHAPTER 8

A Change of Heart

Violet stopped for a moment under the gleaming gold sign, *Archer Brothers Prescription Spectacle Makers* to catch her breath. She was about to push open the polished wooden door when a sudden thought hit like a brick to the head.

Her mother was right. She had IDDCS. She had never heard of it before, but in that moment, she was one hundred percent sure she had it. Of course she was a disobedient child, Mrs. Moody was right. Beatrice, how could she have been so mean to Beatrice, breaking the rules like that in the middle of the school yard. Embarrassing. The pencil, she blushed as she thought about the pencil. Bending down under the desk like that without even thinking of asking teacher, what must the class have thought. She really was a bold child but all that was going to change. She turned around and walked straight back home.

With each stride her new thinking got weaker and by the time she'd reached her home she'd changed her mind again and was back to herself. She sat down on the steps and tried to work out what had happened. Her change of mind had been so quick it scared her.

"THE PILLS!" she shouted jumping up so fast she knocked off her glasses.

Her world went fuzzy. Quickly she sat back down and felt around for the frames. Her hand moved faster as the panic of losing her sight took hold. Suddenly something stirred close by.

"Don't take the pills," a voice whispered in her ear.

She just turned to face the voice when footsteps raced towards her. She was knocked from her spot onto the gravel below scraping her hands and knees. There was a scramble around her and she crawled away as fast as a blind person could. She'd just reached the grassy edge of the lawn when the voice spoke again.

"Here," he said, shoving her glasses into her hand.

Then there was a rush towards the bushes behind the house. Violet lay still for a while. When all the commotion stopped she put back on her glasses. The yard was empty. Maybe she was going mad. She turned over her hands, her palms were bloody. Her school tights were torn and her knees were bloody too. She got up from the grass and dusted off her uniform. She had to find her Dad. There was something going on in Perfect and she needed to convince him to leave. She had proof now, bloody knees and palms should be enough to get his attention. She headed off on her third trip of the afternoon and marched back towards the Archers shop.

This time she didn't stop outside, she turned the polished brass knob and pushed open the door. A bell tingled above to announce her. The shop was empty.

"Mr. Archers," she called.

There was no reply so she took a look around. The shop amazed her just as it had done the first time. The rich browns and golds shone brighter than anything her mother polished and her mother polished a lot in Perfect.

Violet ran her fingers across the walls as she explored. When they danced over an unusual bump in the smooth cherry wood she stopped for closer inspection. There was a thin break in the wood from ceiling to floor dividing the wall in two. She pushed on one of the panels and the wall gave way to a narrow hall behind. Quickly she slipped through the gap. She heard voices coming from behind a door at the end of the hall and tiptoed towards them. It was the Archers. They were fighting. There was a third voice too and she was sure it was her father's. The fight sounded ugly, she hated hearing adults fight.

She didn't want to disturb them so quietly she tiptoed back towards the gap.

"Violet Brown!"

She turned quickly and stood nose to nose with Edward Archer.

"I'm sorry Mr. Archer, I heard voices and I was looking for my Dad. I thought it was him," she stuttered.

"How did you find that door young lady?" Edward Archer said, nodding behind her.

"Oh I wasn't snooping. It was an accident I was just looking around the shop and I found it. I thought Dad might be in here."

"He's just stepped out Violet. I'm afraid you've missed him."

"But I heard him, he was talking to you in there," she pointed behind the stout man.

"Mrs. Moody was right, you really are quite the handful," Edward Archer smiled.

"I em...I'm sorry Mr. Archer," Violet said, stepping slowly backwards, "I must have imagined it."

"What happened you Violet?" Edward Archer asked, taking in her untidy appearance.

"Oh I fell. It's nothing,"

"Violet have you taken your pills dear?"

She stepped back further.

"Your mother told me," he smiled, as if reading her mind, "It's a serious condition Violet, it mustn't go untreated."

"Did William have it too?" she snapped, suddenly filled with anger.

She clasped her hands to her mouth. Edward Archer glared at her. His ferocious anger made him seem bigger.

"What's going on here?" George Archer said, stepping into the hallway behind his brother.

"Nothing," Edward barked, still glaring at Violet, "Violet was looking for her Dad. She's just leaving."

"Oh I'm afraid you've just missed him dear," George Archer smiled, walking to his brother's side.

"Okay thanks," Violet replied, then quickly turned and ran.

Once outside and a safe distance from the shop, she stopped to breathe. Edward Archer scared her. She shouldn't have brought up William. She didn't know what had happened to him. Maybe he'd died, though Edward had looked more angry than sad.

Avoiding home, she walked towards town. The past few hours jumbled in her mind. Maybe she really was going mad, the endless sunny days affecting her mind as well as her sight. First it was her mother and the pills, then her strange change of heart, her glasses, the voice and finally the Archers and their odd behaviour. Worst of all she was certain it was her father's voice she'd heard in the Archers shop. Why didn't they tell her the truth? Had they done something terrible to her Dad?

She walked round the old town, head down avoiding the faces of Perfect. She had no friends and now it seemed she was losing her family. Her parents were all she had. They weren't like normal parents either, not in the way other children's parents were. They gave out to her if she was bold but usually they were great, more like friends than parents. Perfect had changed all that.

Violet knew she couldn't go home. If she went home her mother wouldn't listen. She used to listen. Before they could sit for hours talking about anything but since moving to Perfect things had changed. Her mother didn't notice her anymore. She didn't notice anything.

Her Dad wouldn't listen either. He used to be great fun, always playing tricks. Her Mam said he was a big kid. Violet agreed because most of the time she couldn't tell the difference between her Dad and the boys in her class. Since moving he was angry a lot. He'd be angry with her now for sneaking around the Archers. He was also strict when it came to manners and Violet hadn't been at all mannerly to Edward Archer.

She definitely couldn't go home. She saw a bench and sat down to get her bearings. She'd been in this street before. On the wall almost directly opposite sat a sign *The Birth Place of Messrs George, Edward and William Archer, first sons of Perfect.* It rested on the only house in the town that didn't look quite so clean.

CHAPTER 9

Iris Archer

The house was painted light blue like the sea in pictures of foreign countries. It was in disrepair compared to the other houses on the street.

Violet's heart skipped suddenly when she saw an old lady watching her from behind one of the murky windows. Quickly she looked away. When she looked back the lady was gone. A few minutes later the door of the house swung open and the old woman took back her place at the window. Was she inviting her in? Maybe the old woman knew something about William. What more could go wrong anyway? She stood up from the bench and walked towards the house.

"Hello," she called, stopping just outside the door.

There was no response so she stepped into the hall. The house was as worn inside as it was out. The floor was covered in wonky wood that creaked with every step. Dust gathered thickly on everything in sight. The place was lit by the light that seeped through dirty lace curtains making everything look grey. Dust hit Violet's nostrils and she stifled a sneeze. A door was partially open into the room on her left.

"Hello," she said, pushing it in a little more.

The old lady was sitting in her spot by the window, a shadow cast across half her body.

"You opened the door," Violet said, edging further in.

"I did."

"Are you ok? Do you need some help?"

"No," the old lady croaked.

She had long white hair that fell thinly to the floor, the bottom of it was browned by dirt. Her dress was worn but looked as if it may have been amazing in another life. The colours now muted were just a memory of a bright past. Barefoot and her thin boney feet poked out from under a frayed hem. Her face was kind though she had sad eyes.

"Are you sure you're okay?" Violet asked.

The old woman didn't answer and turned once more to stare out the window. Then it hit Violet.

"You're not wearing glasses?" she gasped.

"Eyes don't need glasses to see. They are the window

to my soul, I will not curtain them."

"But...," Violet stuttered, "how are you not blinded by the sun?"

"It's the sons that's robbed me."

Violet stepped closer.

"Eyes mad," the old woman snapped, a warning."Eyes mad. Them sons makes eyes mad. Iris Archer, they all say, that son's no good. I protected him from Arnold, my William, my apple. Then jealous Ed and Georgie ate him."

"William Archer?" Violet asked, "is he your son?"

"My son, my moon and my stars," Iris replied picking her hair from the floor to wipe her tears.

"I'm sorry," Violet said, "I didn't mean to upset you."

"He's not here," Iris continued, "They said he was bold as brass, a divided soul but I knew he had spirit. A child without spirit is the sky without stars. He had stars my William. A world full of stars. Are you in school with him?"

Violet shook her head.

"No. No I don't go to school with him but my Dad works for George and Edward."

"George and Edward, Edward and George. They took the light from my eyes. They've a streak like their father. All in order, there must be order."

Violet stepped back towards the main door. The old lady was crazy and she didn't want to upset her anymore than she already had.

"Em...my Mam has tea on and I have to go," she mumbled.

"Don't drink the tea," Iris snapped, "don't drink it I tell ya!"

"Em... I won't, I promise," Violet said, edging closer to the door.

She was just about to step out into the hallway when the old lady spoke again. This time she didn't sound so mad.

"You remind me of him Violet. You remind me of my William. There's spirit inside you. Keep it close."

"You know my name?"

"The boy told me. He's watching out for your spirit. You've connected with his soul."

"What boy?"

She hadn't met any boys in Perfect except for the ones in her class and they definitely weren't looking out for her. Iris didn't answer, she had slipped back into her own world. Violet asked once more and with still no luck walked from the house into the perpetual Summer back towards home.

CHAPTER 10

An Urgent Meeting

Her mother was back by the time Violet returned home, and full of the joys of Perfect, she just couldn't stop describing Mrs Bickory's apple pie.

"The best I have ever tasted Violet. I promise I'll make it for you. June gave me the recipe. It's a family secret but she said she would share it with me. Everybody is so nice in this town."

Violet nodded as she took out her schoolbooks.

"Oh good," her mother smiled, "those pills are working. I have never seen you so eager to study dear."

Violet was silent. She wasn't anymore or less eager to study than she had been before but her mother seemed happy and hopefully that meant no more pills.

"Here dear," her mother said, dropping a yellow capsule onto the table, "time for your medication."

"But Mam please I'm fine on the blue ones. I love Perfect," Violet smiled.

"That's great Violet I'm delighted you love it here but that's got nothing to do with your IDDCS. You do want to be cured don't you dear?"

"Can we wait for Dad to come home? Please."

"Okay but your Dad agrees with me. We both want you to be rid of this syndrome. It's holding you back. Think of how much you could achieve without it."

Violet smiled, turned back to her books and pretended to study while Rose Brown whistled the evening away preparing risotto. Violet had never even heard of risotto before Perfect, now it was her mother's speciality.

Hours swept by and her Dad had not returned from work. He never missed dinner. In all the years he had been her father and that was all her life, he had never spent an evening away without telling them. She glanced up at the clock as her mother set the table.

"We can't wait any longer Violet dear," her mother sighed, "this apple pie will go soggy."

"But what about Dad?"

"Don't worry about your father, he can have my pie another day."

"I'm not worried about your pie Mam! Where is Dad? It's not like him to come home late. What if something's happened?"

"In Perfect Violet!" her mother laughed, "Of course nothing has happened to Dad. He's just caught up in his work. He has the best job in the world working with the Archer brothers."

"But Mam," Violet pleaded, "I thought you didn't like the Archers. The first night we came here you said they gave you the..."

"Violet!" her mother snapped running for the pill bottle, "stop being so disruptive, I know it's the syndrome dear but it is getting out of hand. I have never nor will I ever speak of the Archers in such a way."

Quickly she spilled more yellow tablets onto the table. Violet looked at the pills then back at her mother.

"Now!" her mother snapped.

Slowly Violet picked up two canary capsules and placed them under her tongue. Her mother filled a glass with water and handed it to her.

"Swallow," she barked.

Violet did as she was told. Her mother smiled, cleaned up the remaining tablets and resumed dishing out dinner. When her back was turned Violet quickly spat out the pills and shoved them in her pocket.

"Now," her mother smiled a little later, while tucking into her risotto, "I bet you feel better already."

Violet nodded. If she spoke she wouldn't be able to hide the teary tremble in her voice. Oblivious, her Mam chatted about her day right through dinner and dessert.

By late that night her father still hadn't returned and Violet's stomach climbed right into her neck. She felt sick thinking about her visit to the Archers shop. She'd definitely heard her father's voice. Why didn't she question the Archers more? Why did she walk away? Something had to be wrong. Her father was in trouble. Guilt took over as she climbed the stairs to bed.

Just as she reached the top step, the phone rang. She paused. Moving closer to the banisters she sat down and listened.

"Hello," her mother said, in her phone voice.

"Oh Mr. Archer. How can I help you?"

"Yes I thought as much, Violet here was worried."

"She was? Oh really she didn't tell me that."

"I apologise if she upset you Mr. Archer, as I'm sure you've heard she's been diagnosed with IDDCS."

"Yes she's taking the pills. I watched her myself this evening."

"Oh of course Mr. Archer I know how children can be. I'll personally see to it myself."

"Thank you for letting me know about Eugene Mr. Archer. I hope he's helping your research?"

"That's great to hear. How long will he be away?"

"That's great. Thanks for letting me know."

"Yes I'll tell her. Goodnight Mr. Archer."

Why had the Archers rung to tell them her Dad was away? Surely her Dad could pick up the phone? Why couldn't he ring them?

"Violet!" her mother snapped, pulling her daughter from her thoughts, "were you eavesdropping?"

"Oh no I was...I just wanted to hear if it was Dad."

"It was Edward Archer," her mother smiled, "Your

father's going to be away for a few days. He's gone to an optician's conference. Very important apparently."

"Don't you think he would have told us that himself?" Violet said, her voice louder than she'd intended.

"Violet please you are giving me a headache. Edward Archer rang and kindly kept us informed. Your father had to leave quickly. It was urgent."

"An urgent optician's conference?!"

"Violet! This condition is really getting the better of you. It's exhausting dear. Edward Archer was kind enough to enquire after your health. Everyone in this town is being so helpful and you repay them by being ungrateful. I know you were in the Archers shop today."

"I was looking for Dad." Violet snapped.

"You were snooping around in places you shouldn't be. Edward Archer was very good to tell me and he said he wouldn't get the police involved."

"The police?" Violet protested, "but I didn't..."

"Violet," her mother sighed, "enough is enough, just be glad the Archers are so understanding. I'm sure your Dad won't be when he comes home."

Violet didn't respond. There was no point. No matter what she said it would get twisted. She rose from her spot, turned and walked down the carpeted hallway to her room. She locked the door and collapsed onto her bed.

Her world was crashing down around her. Her mother didn't listen and her father had disappeared. She'd been more than mean to him over the last few weeks and now she'd never see him again. She cried until she had no tears left.

She knew the Archers were behind everything, but even if she could prove it no one would listen. It was as if everyone in Perfect was under a spell. Exhausted she crawled in under her duvet and hoped that sleep would find her.

CHAPTER 11

Boy

That night, no matter what, Violet couldn't sleep. There was a strange lump in her bed. After hours of tossing and turning she got up to investigate.

On close inspection she found a thin tear along the top of her mattress. It was about the length of her arm from her elbow to her wrist. She poked her fingers inside, finding there was enough room for her hand she squeezed it through until her fingers brushed off something solid. She pulled the mysterious object from it's hiding place.

The small, flat box fit neatly in her hand. It was dark blue and covered in a bendy ladder like pattern. As she turned the box over the ladders caught the light giving off a silvery sheen. There was a faded stamp on the cover with the words "Optical Prescriptions". The box was closed on one side by a small magnet and rusted hinges held firm the other. Slowly she prised it open. The prettiest pair of glasses sat proud on dark blue velvet interior.

The frames were made of wood and she'd never seen wooden frames before. The lenses were oval and the arms of the glasses were flexible to bend round the ear. They looked as if they came from another world. A label, browned by time, sat centre inside the lid. It read *Optical Prescription Spectacle Makers, 135 Wickham Terrace*. She'd never heard of Wickham Terrace. She took off her specs and fitted the new pair. It was strange, she could see. The lenses suited her perfectly. She was just scanning past the curtains when a figure caught her eye.

"Ah!" she screamed, throwing the glasses from her face.

The room went blurry and she scrambled for her normal specs.

"You saw me?" a voice shouted.

Violet grabbed her duvet and pulled it quickly up over her head. The duvet flew from her grasp and fell to the floor.

"You saw me?" the voice shouted again.

"I didn't. I didn't," Violet shivered, "I didn't see anything. I'm not talking to anyone."

"You did! You saw me," the voice sounded ecstatic, "You saw me standing by the curtains. Wohoo!"

Violet bobbed from side to side as if someone was jumping on her bed.

"The glasses, it has to be the glasses," the voice said again.

There was a scramble through the room.

"Here put them back on."

Her hand was pulled open and the glasses were shoved back into her grip.

"Please put them on," the voice said, "I promise I won't hurt you."

He sounded sincere and Violet had heard this boy's voice before. Slowly she moved the glasses towards her face and pulled the arms around her ears once more. She kept her eyes shut.

"Please," the voice said again.

Wind swished past her face as if someone moved their hands back and forth in front of her. Slowly she opened her eyes.

There at the edge of the bed stood a boy.

He looked straight at her. Twelve maybe thirteen and dressed head to toe in black, he looked like the teenagers her friend Emma talked about. They called themselves Moths or

something like that. He had jet black hair that flopped round his ears and his white face was dappled in tiny freckles mostly gathered round his nose. His eyes were deep navy almost black like the sky at night. Something about them unsettled her.

"You do, you see me," he said, jumping into the air.

A smile filled the boy's face and Violet couldn't help but laugh, he had the most contagious smile she'd ever seen. They stared silently at each other and a little awkwardness flooded the room. Violet tried hard not to blush as she racked her bed brain for something to say.

"I'm Boy," the stranger said, breaking silence.

"I'm Violet," Violet replied, shaking his extended hand, "Is your name really boy?"

"Yes," Boy nodded.

"But that's not a name."

"Yes it is. I've always been called Boy. It's my name like yours is Violet."

"But do your parents call you Boy? They must call you something like Paul or Brian. I knew a few boys from home and none of them were called Boy. They all had names."

"I don't have parents," he smiled.

"Oh!"

There was a little silence and unsure of what to say next Violet copied what adults said at funerals.

"I'm sorry for your loss."

"I didn't lose them," Boy laughed, "I never had parents!"

"You can't never have had parents," Violet replied, "Everybody has parents!"

"Well I don't and as far as I'm concerned I'm better off. Look how yours treat you!"

"Hey," Violet said annoyed, "don't say that about my parents. They're the best anyone could ever have."

"Then why have you been crying for the last few hours. Don't deny it, I saw you."

She fell silent and looked away.

"I didn't mean to upset you Violet," Boy said, "It's just I've been watching you for a while and I know your parents are changing."

"What do you mean?"

"They're changing. It's this place, it does that to people. I've watched every new person that came here and it's happened to them all. After a while they all change. Except you."

"What do you mean change?" Violet asked, though she knew what he meant.

"Well everyone is normal when they get here," Boy replied, "they can see me. I've even had conversations with some newcomers then after a day or two, they start to change. First I'm ignored, then they begin to change their clothes, their hair, the way they talk, even the way they walk and all of a sudden they become like everyone else in this town."

"I know," Violet whispered, "My mam has changed since we've moved here. She was never like this at home. I can't talk to her anymore."

"It's the glasses," Boy said bluntly.

"What do you mean? Without the glasses I can't see."

"But without them you can see," Boy replied, "you can see reality, it's just a little fuzzy. Haven't you noticed all the times you've heard my voice it's when you're not wearing them. Then when you put them on I disappear.

I bet you thought you were going mad!"

"But how can I see you now?"

"I don't know I think it has something to do with those," he said, pointing to the new specs perched on her face.

"I don't know how they work but they work and that's all I care about. It's not easy being invisible."

"I knew it," Violet said sitting upright, "it's my Dad! He must have left them here."

"But why would he do that?" Boy asked.

"I don't know," Violet shrugged, "maybe it's a message. I think he's in some sort of trouble. I have to help him. Maybe he's trying to tell me something."

"I think you're a little dramatic," Boy laughed, grabbing her hand. "Come on, there's something I want to show you."

"Can't it wait until morning?"

"No it can't it has to be at night. They patrol in the day."

"Who patrols?"

"You'll see," Boy winked as he threw Violet's clothes at her and ran out the door.

CHAPTER 12

No Mans Land

"Come on they'll be coming on duty soon and if they catch us we're in trouble." Boy said, when Violet joined him downstairs.

"Who are they? I'm not going anywhere until you tell me, especially if they're as scary as you're saying."

"Ssh keep your voice down Violet," Boy said, gently opening the main door, "they're the Watchers of Perfect. They make sure people like me don't turn up places we shouldn't be."

"Are there more like you?"

"Lots more," Boy smiled slipping outside.

Violet followed him out onto the dark doorstep.

"But it wouldn't matter, we can't see you anyway," she whispered.

"What if someone's glasses fell off in the middle of the

day and suddenly they could hear all these invisible people talking?"

"Well maybe they'd just think they were going mad. I think everyone in this town is mad."

"Maybe you're the one who's mad," Boy smiled crossing the gravel to take a short cut through the lawn.

"I'm not mad." Violet snapped.

"That's what all mad people say!"

Violet shoved her elbow into Boy's side.

"Hey what's that for?"

"For all the mad people," she laughed and ran ahead.

Boy gave chase and before long they found themselves on the edge of town. Suddenly he grabbed Violet's hand and yanked her back.

"You have to be careful," he whispered, looking around, "we can't get caught."

Violet was scared but not wanting Boy to think she was a girly girl she followed him silently into the town. Perfect was eerie in the darkness and not half as neat as it looked in the daylight. Paint was chipped and worn from buildings, hanging baskets weren't as full or colourful and rubbish even whistled past her feet down the empty street.

"It doesn't look like the same place," she whispered, sticking closely to Boy's side.

"It's not the same place really. Well it is and it isn't," he replied.

A chill ran up her spine as they passed through the town square and onto one of the smaller side roads. She stopped suddenly. A figure moved on the ground just up ahead.

"Don't be such a chicken," Boy laughed.

Nobody would call her a coward! She moved shoulder to shoulder with Boy.

"You know you can't be out this far Paddy," Boy said gently nudging the feet of the slumped figure.

An ancient man looked up and into Violet's eyes. He had a long beard, which was matted and black with dirt. His clothes fell loosely from his scrawny frame and a battered hat clung awkwardly to the side of his head.

"I don't care 'bout them Boy," he said waving a dismissive hand at the pair, "what more can they do.

Now be gone with ye and don't be hasslin me."

"He's always like that," Boy whispered, as he nodded and walked past, "doesn't ever obey rules. That's the thing with my people, rules don't really exist."

"What do you mean your people?" Violet asked.

"The outcasts. The exiles. The unwanted, we've lots of names," Boy smiled, "we're the mayhem of Perfect. You'll see."

As they walked further down people began to fill up the lane. They were carrying all sorts, rushing this way and that as if it were the middle of the day and not the dead of night. Violet clung to Boy's sleeve afraid she'd lose him in the crowd.

"What are they doing?" she whispered.

"Working of course."

"But at night?"

"Your night is our day. It's the only time we can walk through Perfect. Once daylight arrives the Watchers are on strict patrol. Then no one is safe."

"What do you do then?"

"Me? Well I follow you."

"What do you mean you follow me?" Violet snapped.

"Ssh," he laughed, pointing ahead.

Violet followed his finger until her eyes landed on the strangest gates she'd ever seen.

They were huge, in both height and width. Made from barbed wire, which was twisted and wrapped to form the enormous pillars, they looked angry. The steel was rusted in places so hints of orange and gold decorated the grey metal. The words: *No Man's Land* made from more twisted wire rested proudly above the pillars forming the gateway.

Bits and bobs of everything were skewered to the barbed teeth. Paper, material, flowers and ribbons wrapped the gates in colour taking the edge off their scary image. Some of the items were worn and torn like they'd hung on the pillars forever, while others looked shiny and new.

A faded red ribbon caught Violet's eye fluttering in the gentle night breeze. Words were delicately sewn into the material. *For the memories I lost to Perfect. I will never forget you Mam. Your loving daughter Pip.*

"Pippa Moody," Boy whispered.

"Mrs. Moody?"

"Yeah," he nodded, "Pip was your teacher's daughter. We call these the Rag Gates. The people of No Man's

Land leave messages on them for the ones they've lost. I think they hope that some day their families might come looking for them. I think it's stupid. Nobody's coming for us."

"But?"

"There are lots more like Pippa. She's not the only one lost to Perfect."

"What age was she?"

"I think she was twelve when they brought her here. She's a lot older now, like twenty or something."

"But why do they take children?" Violet asked, "what about their parents? Don't they notice they're gone?"

"No. Like you said it's almost as if they're not their parents anymore. Something happens to them in Perfect. I don't know what but I think it has something to do with the glasses."

"What happened to Pippa?"

"She was disobeying the rules. Nothing serious, but you know small things are big in Perfect. One night they came to her house and took her. She went back loads of times to see if her family would help but she was invisible to them. Soon they forgot all about her."

"But what if that happens to me?" Violet stammered, "Is it only children they take? Maybe they took my Dad."

"It won't happen to you, well not yet," Boy smiled, "I don't think your Dad is here anyway, there are adults too but most were taken as children. Adults fall under Perfect's spell a lot easier. They seem to like the rules."

"Why?" Violet asked, as they walked through the gates.

Boy shrugged and sprinted ahead.

"Too many questions Violet. Let's have some fun. Come on there's lots to do here and not very much time to do it."

Violet looked around. She'd passed through the gates into a different world, a circus world.

Straight in front of her was an overgrown park, the grass was about knee high and full of daisies and dandelions. Surrounding the park was a jumble of odd houses, some tall and wobbly, others short and squat. Made mostly of wood and cardboard, they crowded each other out so windows sat against neighbours walls and rooftops touched off rooftops. Large nails dotted the houses like rusty patterns holding whole streets together. Around the base of the tightly packed buildings ran poky laneways.

Violet's foot hit off something solid. A man sprawled unconscious on the road in front of her was blocking the path. His shirt had no buttons and hung loose exposing his hairy bare belly. As she was jumping over him, another man pushed by her in a hurry. He was dressed in a top hat and tails over a pair of red and white striped pyjamas. He held a cane in one hand and an enormous branch of a tree in the other. Just behind him a lady wearing a bright blue ball gown puffed and panted as she pedalled a tricycle over the pot holed road.

"Excuse me, late for the theatre," she roared, as she raced past.

Violet jumped out of the way and hit off the side of one of the houses. It wobbled above her. Quickly she darted down a nearby laneway after Boy hoping that the building wouldn't fall. They spent the rest of the night exploring the madness of No Mans Land.

It was definitely madness. Every turn they took something was happening. Some streets were lined with rundown shops, the glass so cracked and dirty that Violet couldn't see what they were selling. Others were packed with stalls where dodgy men and women gathered to sell all sorts. Winks and nods passed between the stall owners like their own silent language. Dirty children ran barefoot through the crowds without any adults to mind them. Some were in gangs while others hung round on their own. A thin girl stole an apple from a stall in front of them. When the owner spotted it, he gave chase through the lane knocking over everything in his path.

"What will happen to her?"

Violet pointed pulling on Boy's shirt sleeve.

"There are some rules here, they're street rules. They're not written down or anything but everybody knows them. If he catches her, she'll get what she deserves."

"He won't kill her will he?"

Boy laughed sprinting ahead. He skimmed his hand over the stalls as he passed and when they rounded the corner up ahead he stopped and picked two buns from his pocket.

"Let's hope they don't kill thieves," he laughed, scoffing down one as he handed the other to Violet.

"But that's stealing Boy. You can't steal from people!"

"You sound like a Perfect girl," Boy mumbled.

"I am not!"

"Well eat it then," he laughed.

She looked at the bun then back at her friend. Wiping the smile from his face she bit deep into the spongy core.

"No one's gonna take care of you here Violet," Boy said, "You have to look out for yourself. Come on. I'll bring you home. The Watchers will be out soon and if they catch you here there'll be real trouble."

CHAPTER 13

The Watchers

Violet grabbed Boy's hand and they raced back through the narrow streets in the direction they had come. The sun was just rising over the dilapidated rooftops when they reached the gates. Everyone was making their way back into No Man's Land. Boy stopped at the edge of the street that led into Perfect and signalled Violet to stay back while he peered round the corner. Then he put his finger to his lips and called her forward.

"You have to be quiet," he whispered, "We're a little late."

Violet tiptoed after her friend. She'd never seen a Watcher but if Boy's stories were anything to go by she definitely didn't want to. As quietly as possible, they slipped through the morning shadows up the narrow laneway and out onto the main street of Perfect. All was quiet and Violet's thumping heart relaxed as they reached the edges of the town. They were just passing the Archers when suddenly Boy wrestled her into the nearby bushes.

"Blasted early mornings," a gruff voice said, "he's always late. Expects me to be waiting around for 'im!"

It came from the direction of the Archers. A man paced back and forth outside the front door of the brothers shop. He blew air into his giant, cupped hands to warm them against the morning cold. He was average height and wore black, from the tip of his toes to the top of his head. He was wide and square and not at all perfect.

"Ah what took you so long? You're the last one in!" he shouted over his shoulder.

Another man walked towards the shop from the direction of Violet's house. This man was solid like a brick, very short and was also dressed head to toe in black. He was weighed down by a strange machine strapped tightly to his back and carried a leather notebook under his arm. He looked worried and shook his head from side to side as he handed over the book.

"What do you mean 'no show'?" the waiting man roared as he stared at the opened page.

"I'm sorry Fists, she just wasn't there. I waited for hours!"

"How could she not be there? SHE LIVES THERE! You know what the brothers will say when they hear about this. She's top of the list; get your thick head around

88

that. She needs to be zapped!"

"I know but she wasn't there, I couldn't do anything about it. I swear. I got her mother though. Please don't tell the brothers," the other man pleaded.

"Give me the zapper. If you want a job done right you have to do it yourself!" Fists said as he grabbed the strange backpack from the other man.

"But, but it's almost daylight..."

"Shut up and get home. I don't give a damn what time it is. I'll get her, you mark my words and then we'll see what the brothers have to say about this!"

The smaller man stood shivering outside the door of the spectacle shop as he watched Fists stride away from the town.

"Watchers?" Violet whispered.

Boy nodded.

"We need to get you home Violet," he whispered a few moments later, "I think that's where Fists is headed."

"To my house?"

"Yes. Come on."

Quickly he pulled Violet off the ground and they raced from the bushes.

"I'm going to cause a diversion," Boy panted as they sprinted along the road. "Don't worry about me, you have to get into your house but don't go to bed. Put on your uniform as if you're ready for school then go downstairs and act as normal as possible. Make sure you put on your old glasses. Don't worry, if Fists does pay a visit you won't notice a thing."

"Why would he pay a visit?"

"Just do it!" Boy said sharply pulling her faster along the road.

They were just around the corner from her house when they spotted Fists a little ahead. The pair jumped over a low wall and followed him as quietly as they could through the cover of the trees that lead into Violet's garden.

"Right. Go. Now," Boy whispered.

Suddenly he turned and raced towards Fists. Violet sprinted for her house. A painful cry echoed behind her but she didn't look back. Her legs were on fire. She darted through the trees, across the gravel and up the stone steps. She scrambled for the keys her mother always left under the potted plant, opened the door and rushed up the stairs to her room. She threw on her uniform and ran two steps at a time back down to the kitchen. Trying to catch her breath, she opened the fridge door to get milk for her breakfast.

Just then there were footsteps in the kitchen. She froze. All air flew from her lungs. Act normal, act normal. As calmly as possible she picked up the milk, closed the fridge door and turned to walk back towards the table. He was there. Right in front of her. His black eyes bore into hers. Her heart beat at rapid speed. The glasses. She'd forgotten to take off the glasses. It was too late, if she took them off now he would know. She had to pretend she didn't see him.

Looking straight ahead she walked towards the table. He was in her way but she couldn't veer around him. Keeping on course she prayed he would move. Just a step away from a crash, Fists slipped aside, his eyes still firmly fixed on her. She tried to hide her relief as she sat down and shakily poured a bowl of cereal. For distraction she picked up the cereal box and studied the back. Her eyes scanned the words but didn't take in a single one as Fists moved his face so close she could smell his stinking breath.

After a while he stepped back and, as if remembering something, quickly left the room and headed upstairs.

He was light on his feet and Violet strained to hear what room he entered. A few moments later he was back in the kitchen. Again she acted as normal as possible, cleared up her place and took out some schoolbooks. Looking frustrated, Fists left the house a little later.

Waiting a few minutes to make sure he was gone, Violet ran as fast as she could up the stairs and into her mother's room.

"Mam, Mam, are you alright?" she stuttered, shaking her mother's lifeless figure.

"Violet, for goodness sake. What time is it?" her mother slurred sleepily.

"You're alright," Violet sighed, throwing her arms round her.

"Violet dear off course I'm alright, whatever has gotten into you?"

"Nothing Mam, I just em...I just had a bad dream."

"You and your imagination," her mother smiled, rubbing her hair. "Are those new glasses pet?"

"Oh yeah. I em... I got them free in school. I'll...I'll make you breakfast." Violet said, quickly running out the door.

Back in her bedroom she found her old glasses and put them on. Placing the new ones in their box she shoved them back into their hiding place in the mattress and returned downstairs to make her mother's breakfast.

CHAPTER 14

A Night Visitor

All day in school Violet ran through the night's events. She was so distracted Mrs. Moody made her swallow more pills. Violet pretended then spat them out as soon as teacher's back was turned.

Something was up and now she knew the Archers had to be involved. First there was the glasses, something about them neither Boy or Violet understood made the people of Perfect act strange and caused No Man's Land to disappear altogether. Then there was the Watchers who met up outside the Archer's shop and talked about the brothers. Everything pointed back to Edward and George but Violet couldn't piece together exactly how. She had so many questions, but she needed to find answers.

As the day wore on she became convinced that her Dad was in trouble. He wasn't on a business trip. It was his voice she heard that day in the shop. She needed to talk to Boy.

That evening as the sun fell over Perfect she said goodnight to her Mam and climbed the stairs to her room. Finding the glasses where she'd left them she slipped the box into her pocket and tiptoed back down. Slipping silently past the sitting room where her Mam watched T.V. she slowly opened the front door and stepped outside. The cold evening air made her shiver as she took up a spot on the first step.

Carefully she took the glasses from her pocket, placed her normal pair in the box and put on the new ones. There was no one there, she'd thought maybe Boy would be. She stayed on the spot past darkness waiting for him. Maybe Fists had done something to him, maybe he needed her help. She could go back to No Man's Land, she was worried but without Boy she'd never find the way. It was well into night when she raised her stiff legs and as quietly as possible slipped back inside.

Her mother was long in bed and the lights were off all over the house. She picked her way along the hall and tiptoed up the stairs. She was just at the top when the front door unlocked. Her heart jumped. Quietly she placed her hands on the banisters and peered over. A figure moved slowly through the hallway, too large to be Boy's. As the person got closer she gasped. It was the Watcher from the previous night, the one who'd fought with Fists.

Violet sprung to action. Nerves raced through her veins as she made as quietly as possible for her room. Keeping on her new specs, she took the old ones from her pocket and placed them on the bedside table. She threw on her pyjamas and snuck into bed pulling the sheets right up over her head. She lay still. Her heart pounded in her ears. It wasn't long before her door creaked open. It was stupid to wear the glasses but it was the only way she could find out what the Watcher wanted and maybe help her Dad.

His steps were quiet, how could someone so big make so little noise. He stopped by the edge of the bed, his eyes burning a hole in her sheets. She prayed he couldn't smell fear. There was a faint creak as her glasses case opened. Suddenly a loud noise, like someone sucking snots up their nose, took over the room. Just as quickly it stopped, the box snapped closed and the Watcher slipped quietly from the room.

Violet turned over to check her glasses. They looked normal. The Watchers footsteps left her mothers room, heading back downstairs. She jumped from the bed, forced on her runners and opened the door. Waiting until the Watcher was in the hallway below, she tiptoed after him out of the house, across the yard, through the trees and down the main road towards town. She was near the spot where she'd hidden the previous night when a hand grabbed her.

"What do you think you're doing?" Boy whispered.

"You scared the life out of me!" Violet gasped, catching her breath.

"What do you think you're doing? How stupid are you Violet?"

"I'm following him," she snapped, "there's something up and I need to know what it is. I have to save my Dad."

"What do you mean? What do you think is wrong with your Dad?"

"Well...I don't know really but there's something wrong and I think the Archers are behind it."

"What!" Boy said, his face mocking, "Did you come up with all this today?"

"Yeah and without your help."

"Well you needed my help last night! Where's my thanks for distracting Fists? And I would have been at yours tonight except the Watchers were watching me. Fists wasn't happy that I jumped him you know!"

"Look," Violet said, ignoring Boy, "I knew it. He's going into the Archers. We have to go inside. It's the only way we'll find out what's going on."

"Ah Violet," Boy said, raising an eyebrow, "I might be brave but I'm not stupid. Whatever the Watchers are doing in there you don't want to know."

"I do," Violet protested.

"You don't! You don't know what they are like Violet. You saw No Man's Land; there are places darker than that. Places where the Watchers send people when they want them gone, disappeared, for real. It's not safe Violet. It's not a game."

"I don't think it's a game! I know they have my Dad and I have to save him before Mam forgets he ever existed."

Boy's expression changed. Violet held his gaze. Did he ever miss his Dad? The Dad he said he never had.

"Come on," he said, crawling out from behind the bush and running the shadows towards the Archers shop.

CHAPTER 15

Jars Of Colour

Violet followed silently behind, afraid any minute another Watcher might stumble upon them. Quickly they crossed the distance to the Archers. Boy signalled to stay back while he approached the door. Not listening she was by his side when he discovered it was locked.

"What will we do?" she whispered, causing Boy to jump.

"I told you to stay back."

"He's my Dad!"

"Do you have a hair clip?" he whispered, ignoring her tone.

She pulled a pin from her ponytail. Boy fiddled with the doorknob and after a few minutes it came loose in his hand.

"Have you been to jail?" she whispered.

"No!"

"It's just I thought people only learned that stuff in jail."

"Or No Man's Land." he winked, gently pushing in the door.

The shop was empty and they slipped in, closing the door behind them. Inside was dark and Violet prayed she wouldn't bump into anything.

"There's no one about," Boy whispered, after a quick investigation, "they're not here Violet. Now let's go, I don't like the feeling I get in this place."

"Please Boy, just a few more minutes. I want to check something. I have an idea where Dad might be. Then I promise I'll leave."

Reluctantly he agreed. Quickly Violet ran her fingers along the mahogany walls until she hit a familiar bump. Pushing it just a little the wall gave way to the secret passage. She smiled at Boy and entered.

It was dark, even darker than the shop floor as there were no windows. A thin strip of light warmed the carpet on the opposite wall marking another doorway. A shadow passed through the light. Violet inched her way across the room, and placed her ear against the dark wood. A familiar sound greeted her, a sucking noise. She pulled Boy alongside to listen. After a few minutes it stopped and the light went out.

"Do you know the noise?" Violet whispered.

Boy shook his head.

> "I heard it tonight in my house. I think it's from the machine the Watcher carries on his back. We have to go in there."

> "No we don't," Boy protested, "you don't know what you're saying. You're new here but you should be afraid of the Watchers. They're dangerous Violet."

> "Please Boy," she begged, "You have no parents so maybe you don't understand but my Dad is one of my two favourite people in the world. I can't let anything happen to him. I need to find out what's going on."

Boy stepped back from the door and sat down. Violet bit her lip. She shouldn't have said what she'd said. Her Dad always told her to think before she speaks otherwise she might hurt people's feelings just like she's hurt Boy's.

> "I'm sorry I didn't mean it," she whispered, sitting down beside her friend.

> "I'm not afraid of the Watchers you know."

> "I know you're not."

> "Well let's go in then." Boy said, pushing off the floor.

"Boys," Violet sighed, they never made any sense.

Listening again to make sure there was no one in the room beyond, Boy leaned his weight against the door. It began to move. He opened it just enough for the pair to slip through, then shut it quietly behind.

Violet stood just inside the entrance. It wasn't a room at all. It was more like a long, narrow hallway. Steel shelving ran the length of both walls standing about five feet high. It looked odd compared to the beautiful wood in the rest of the shop. The shelves were filled with rows upon rows of glass jars. Each jar held a strange coloured gas that glowed in the dark of the room.

"What are they?" Violet whispered, picking up a jar.

The gas was dull, a dark blue green colour that moved sluggishly inside it's glass. Beside her Boy was holding another jar with slightly brighter colours, dark blue greens mixed with hints of yellow and a single stream of bright red.

"Look," Boy whispered, shoving his jar into Violet's face.

A worn sticker on top of the jar read *Mr. John Bumsbury. Completed 09th Dec 1983.* Violet looked up at her friend.

"Haven't a clue," he shrugged.

She moved her jar towards Boy's for a little more light then read the lid.

"Mrs. Charlotte Cotts. Completed 24th March 1970. That's ancient," she whispered.

"Come on," Boy said, leaving down his jar.

He walked towards the far end of the room not stopping until he reached a separate section of shelving. The jars here were different. They were only partially full, the gas was brightly coloured, almost luminous and moved rapidly through the confined space. The mixtures of colour were beautiful. Boy picked one up, *Mr. Jim Joiners. Incomplete. Last Session 14th June 1985. NML.*

"I know him," he said, his voice shaky, "he lives in No Man's Land."

Quickly he put it down and picked another, *Mr. Raymond Splinters. Incomplete. Last Session 01st Aug 2001. NML.*

"I know him too."

Violet was reaching for another jar when a noise startled the pair. Quickly they ran for cover. Violet dived for the bottom of the shelf she was standing beside. Pushing some jars out of the way she crawled in towards the back. Suddenly the lights flickered on.

Footsteps advanced down the hallway towards her hiding place. A pair of large, polished, brown, leather shoes walked past, stopping millimeters from where she knelt hiding.

"Ah Violet Brown," George Archer suddenly said, "I hope you've been a good girl."

Her heart stopped. How had he found her? She waited in disbelief for the giant to bend down and grab her but he appeared to be distracted by some jars on the shelf above.

"That blasted Watcher!" he spat, "Still not enough. Do I have to do everything myself?"

Glass clattered angrily off glass and George Archer turned on his heels and marched down to the other end of the hallway. The lights switched off, a door slammed and the room was plunged back into darkness.

"He was looking at that jar," Boy said, jumping out from hiding to run to the spot where George Archer had stood.

Violet crawled out less elegantly from her crouched spot and was by his side to hear him gasp. His hand shook as he held the jar. It was about a quarter full of brightly coloured gas, which raced around at lightening speed. He passed it silently to Violet. She stared, gobsmacked, at the spanking new label.

Miss. Violet Brown. Processing.

She handed the jar back to Boy and slid down the wall onto the floor.

"What is it?" she trembled, "why does it have my name on it?"

"I don't know Violet," Boy whispered, finding her side, "but I promise we'll find out."

CHAPTER 16

The Warning

The pair sat side by side in the darkness too shaken to talk. The Archers were up to something and it involved Violet.

"Come on," Boy smiled, a little later, "No more moping. We're not going to sit around when there's a mystery to be solved."

"What do you mean, I thought you wanted to go back?"

"Well that was before I saw your name on that jar. Nobody can put your name on a jar of colourdy stuff without asking me first."

Violet sighed.

"I don't know Boy. Maybe you were right; maybe I should be more careful."

"That was the old me," Boy said, sounding brave, "Now you are involved in this whole mystery, the jar tells us that. I think we have to find your Dad. If he doesn't know what to do then at least you'll all be back together and can escape from Perfect."

Violet nodded. She trusted Boy. He was almost her best friend already and it had taken her two whole weeks to get to that stage with her old one Becky. Her family had to leave Perfect but maybe, since Boy didn't have any parents, he'd come with them. She wouldn't tell him yet though, families were a touchy subject.

After a quick discussion, Boy did most of the talking as Violet was still a little shaky, they decided to follow George Archer. He was annoyed over Violet's jar and was definitely on a mission so wherever he was going might lead them to her Dad.

They walked the long corridor following George's direction past more rows of shelving, until they reached a dead end. Violet and Boy heard a door bang when George left, but they were now facing a stone wall. Boy ran at it and had to bite his tongue not to cry out in pain when he slammed into the solid structure.

"Well that was a bit stupid," Violet laughed.

"Any better ideas?" Boy snapped, cradling his shoulder.

"I bet it's like the hidden doorways in the Archers shop. I had to run my hands...hold on."

Her fingers slipped across a loose stone. She pulled on the brick and the top half popped out from the wall like a door handle. Violet glanced at Boy, smiled, turned the stone and pushed. The wall gave way to another hall beyond. Quickly the two passed through, gently closing the door behind them.

The hallway was circular and lined in stone, the same sort that the door was made from; solid squares of rock like it was part of a castle. This hallway was very small, more like a landing, and to the left of it was a set of steps that spiralled downwards. The space was lit by a mounted torch, the flickering flame warmed the cold stone. Quickly Boy grabbed the torch from its perch and began to descend the stairs.

"We can only go down," he whispered.

Violet nodded, her bravery was being tested.

"I feel like we're in a computer game," she said, following close behind.

"What's that?"

"You know a computer game. You must have played at least one before you came to Perfect?"

Boy fell silent, just like he'd done before when Violet mentioned his lack of parents. What had she said wrong this time? How could talking about computer games upset anyone?

"Your parents weren't killed by a computer game or anything were they? I heard once before from a girl in school that that had happened to a friend of hers. I'm really sorry Boy, I didn't know."

"No," Boy snapped, "I don't know what a computer game is."

"Oh is that all, well you've spent way too long in Perfect," Violet laughed relieved.

"I never lived in Perfect," Boy whispered, so faintly Violet barely heard him.

"But how did you get to No Man's Land then?"

"I don't know. I was born there I think. I don't ever remember anywhere else."

"Oh!"

What could she say? She didn't want her shock to be obvious but all words disappeared from her brain. They continued the descent without talking, the steps seeming to spiral forever.

"We'll be in the centre of the world soon," she said, to break the silence.

Suddenly Boy jumped back pushing her up against the cold stone. He brought the flame round to his face and put his finger to his lips silencing her protest. He pointed down the stairwell. A chilling cry reached up from below. Someone was in pain, not just ordinary pain, terrifyingly painful pain.

"I promise, I'll get her next time Sir," someone whimpered.

"You better or you know where I'll be sending you," George Archer hissed, "There's too many going to No Man's Land, until Brown fixes our problem I don't want anymore disappearing."

"I understand Sir, it's just this Violet's a hard'ne to crack. I'm doin the same that I do t'all the rest but I think she's got too much."

"I don't care how much she has, just figure it out! I WANT NO MORE DISAPPEARING!!"

"I understand Mr. Archer Sir," the voice trembled, "I'll do me best."

"YOU'LL DO YOUR JOB!"

Footsteps pounded across the floor below. Then, after a few moments of silence, laughter erupted.

"I'll do me best Mr. Archer Sir!" a different voice snorted.

"Well what was I meant to say?"

"I love you Mr. Archer Sir," someone else sniggered.

Boy whispered to Violet to stay put. Then he quenched the flame with his foot and followed the stairwell down. Violet stood in the darkness. She fought the urge to run listening to the voices squabble below. What did the Archers want her Dad to fix?

"There's three of them. Watchers," Boy whispered, rejoining her side, "I think they are getting ready to sleep off their night's work. I figure, give them another little while and they'll be out for the count. Then we can move on."

"What about George Archer? Is he still there?"

"No. I didn't see him. There's a few passages leading off the Watchers room. I'd say he went down one of them."

Violet shivered as she sat on the step to wait. She couldn't shut off her imagination, her head swam in terrifying images of what might happen. Sometimes her imagination was her worst enemy but other times it was her best asset, at least that's what her Mam told her. She couldn't think about her Mam. She needed to be strong, not just because she had to rescue her Dad but she had to rescue her Mam too. Boy shifted uncomfortably next to her and she sought out his hand on the cold stone floor.

She slipped her fingers through his and felt safe.

"You know," she whispered, "my parents can be yours too."

There was nothing for a minute. Had she upset him again? Then he squeezed her hand.

CHAPTER 17

Deadly Cold

"Come on," Boy whispered, after an eternity in the dark, "I think they've gone asleep."

Violet got up and, keeping her left hand against the wall, tiptoed after Boy. As they neared the bottom, light trickled up from a doorway below. Violet held her breath; any sound could wake the sleeping Watchers. Boy, a little ahead, entered the room. She followed suit, though every sinew told her to run. She would show Boy she wasn't a girly girl.

The room was large and cold. About twenty rope hammocks dotted the cavernous space hanging from hooks in the stone ceiling. Most were empty except for three, which were occupied by sleeping Watchers oblivious to their intruders. Violet passed a heap of upturned wooden crates in the middle of the room where a card game was laid out ready to play. The place was really messy, lots of large black shirts, enormous black trousers and giant leather boots created obstacles in the middle of the floor. It was definitely a boy's room. Violet held her nose to block out the sweaty stench and picked her way past.

"Down here," Boy whispered, ducking into a passageway.

Though it was dark Boy didn't dare light the torch still held in his grasp, so they moved quickly along keeping close to the wall. They had been travelling a while when they reached a crossroads.

"Which way?" Violet whispered.

"I don't know. Does either of them give you a feeling?"

"What do you mean a feeling?"

"I don't know, like do you think your Dad might be at the bottom of one of them?"

Violet walked to the entrance of the first passage. She stood for a minute, walked down a little then turned and came back. Shrugging she walked to the next entrance.

This time a chill slithered up her spine and grabbed the air from her throat. Arctic winds wrapped her like snake would it's prey, and howled round the space. It was like all her blood had frozen as if she was dead. Terrified she sprinted back to where Boy stood waiting.

"This one," she stuttered, pointing to the first passage, "not the other one. Definitely not the other one."

Boy smiled at her odd behaviour as he followed her down the first passage. They'd been walking for a while when voices reached them from a little ahead. A group of men were approaching from the other direction. The pair frantically searched for a hiding space. The walls were solid. There was nowhere to go. The voices were getting closer, Violet tried not to panic. Thinking quickly Boy grabbed her arm and raced back the way they had come.

"Hey you's!" a voice roared from behind.

Violet's legs turned to lead, her heart was racing but she wasn't moving fast enough. Her pursuer pounded the stones just a few paces behind. With each step he was closer. Suddenly someone grabbed her top, yanking her backwards. She squealed. Boy turned and sprinted towards her, the torch held high. A sharp cry filled the air as he brought the wooden object down heavily on her attacker. Her legs reawakened. Grabbing Boy's hand again they flew back through the passageway. Now the rest of the gang joined the chase and had almost caught up to them when the pair broke onto the crossroads and ducked down the second entrance. Their attackers came to an abrupt stop. Violet looked around unsure she believed her ears.

Three Watchers stood laughing at the top of the tunnel. They remained there mocking for a minute then turned and disappeared. Violet pulled sharply on Boy's hold.

"They've gone Boy. They've stopped," she panted.

"You sure?" he replied running back a little to check.

"I saw them. They stopped when we turned down here. There's something about this place..." she trailed off wrapping her arms tight across her chest to combat the sudden cold.

"We've no choice," Boy said, "We have to go on. We can't go back. They've seen us now."

Violet nodded and followed his lead. The path became extremely dark. She moved closer to her friend. A mist seeped into the tunnel filling the stone space. It's icy tongue licked Violet's skin. She searched out Boy's hand in the darkness. He was shivering.

"Are you okay?" she whispered.

He didn't respond.

"Boy please you're frightening me. Where are we?"

"Do you hear them?" his voice was weak.

"Who?"

Violet moved closer wrapping herself round the top of his arm. Someone was watching them. She looked behind but could see nothing in the thick black.

"Do you hear the voices Violet?"

Boy sounded desperate, urgent.

'What voices? It's just the wind. Please Boy you're scaring me."

"They're crying. I think they're crying Violet."

"Who's crying? Please Boy stop it!"

There was a rustle behind her. Violet panicked. Letting go of Boys arm, she sprinted for the light that trickled into the tunnel ahead. Within moments she broke out into open space and collapsed at the waist to catch her breath. Something creaked loudly and she sprung upright. An old iron gate rose from the mist in front of her. Hanging loosely on it's hinges it swung in the wind.

"See Boy," she said, jumping up and down, "that's what you heard, an old gate!"

He didn't respond, his face was as white as her mother's starched sheets. He was scaring Violet, so to steady her beating heart she ignored him and looked around. The gates hung from two crumbling stone pillars covered in moss and ivy that were part of a surrounding wall. The wall reached to Violet's chin and she had to hoist herself up on her arms to peer over it. Tall stone structures floated in the mist beyond. The gates creaked loudly again pulling Violet's attention.

"No please stop Boy! Don't...it's a graveyard" she stuttered, jumping down from the wall.

He kept walking and had almost disappeared into the fog before Violet followed him. She had no choice. Slowly she pushed open the gate, her heart pounding. A path led through the middle of the graves. It was overgrown in weeds, and to distract her imagination she counted them as she walked past the gravestones.

"1 dandelion, 2 daisies, 2 dandelions...Ouch"

Something sharp ripped through the skin on her forearm. She looked up suddenly and screamed. A dismembered hand sat impaled on a wooden stake. The skin was purpley blue and green pus poured from the maggot-made wounds. A roughly scrawled sign was nailed to the stake below.

KEEP OUT IF YOU KNOW WHAT'S GOOD FOR YOU!

"Please Boy. Please can we leave!" she cried into the fog.

Her fear raised Boy from his trance and he raced back to her side.

"Violet, are you okay? What's wrong?" he panted.

She pointed to the sign just as a shadow moved out from behind a tombstone ahead. Boy grabbed her arm and pulled her roughly down onto the soggy grass, using a stone cross as cover.

"Stay here," he mouthed silently.

She nodded, her voice stolen. Just as Boy was moving she grabbed his sleeve pulling him back.

"I have to check it out," he shivered, shaking her off, "I'll be back in a minute. I promise."

He was gone. She was alone.

'Everything will be okay. Everything will be okay.'

Something brushed off her shoulder. She jumped back suddenly and stumbled to the side before losing her balance. A hand reached up to break her fall and she grabbed for it in the darkness.

"Oh Boy. You scared me," she gasped, turning around.

Hollow eye sockets stared at her from a mutilated skull.

She screamed and darted forwards. Tripping over something she fell into a sea of maggot-ridden bodies. Bones cracked breaking under her weight as she crawled across the masses of dead people. Finding solid ground, she sprinted for the wall that surrounded the graveyard and scrambled over the top into mossy grass on the other side.

A blinking streetlamp yellowed the mist and she stumbled across the balding lawn towards it. As she got closer her fear subsided and her thoughts shifted into a world of problems. Images of rotten skin, maggots and bone flew from consciousness and she became clouded in worry. What if her Mam didn't love her anymore? Maybe it had nothing to do with Perfect, maybe her mother hated her. What if her Dad disappeared on purpose, maybe he had another family or maybe he didn't love her either and that's why he left? She blamed the Archers for everything when really it was her own fault. Her heart sank, pulling heavily on her chest and before she realised it she was on her knees. Every bad thought imaginable ate away at her mind until her life felt bleak and she couldn't see an escape.

She looked around for Boy. The mist had thickened. She couldn't see him. He'd left too, or maybe he'd been attacked in the graveyard and his half eaten body lay with the others. Everyone that meant anything had gone. They'd abandoned her. Pulling her knees towards her, she wrapped her arms around her legs, shielding herself from the outside. Soon the mist cocooned her from the world. She cried. For her Mam and Dad, for the friends she'd lost, for Boy and his lack of parents. She cried for all the things she had ever heard about in school, like the floods in Pakistan, the starving children in Africa, and she cried for herself. This was how Boy found her.

"Violet," he panted, sitting down beside her, "I was looking for you."

She didn't look up. She was angry with him and definitely didn't want him to see her crying.

"Where were you?" she stammered, "You left me."

"I'm sorry," he pleaded, "I didn't leave you. I went to see what the noise was. I thought it was George Archer."

"But you left me, with...those bodies."

"I'm sorry Violet. I didn't know. If I'd known I'd never..." he trailed off.

"Who are they...who did this?" she quivered, rocking back and forth beneath the street lamp.

"I...I don't know Violet."

The pair sat shoulder to shoulder in silence. The mist grew thicker and a distant rumble of thunder filled the skies.

"Violet," Boy whispered a while later, "Please look at me."

"I know," he said, wiping his red eyes, "It's this place. It brings out every bad thing you've ever thought. I heard about it before but I never believed the stories."

"What do you mean?"

"I'll show you," he said, standing up to pull his friend gently from the soggy grass.

They walked together through the mist. Soon large trees loomed out from the fog dotted round a small park. Like winter trees, they had no leaves. Their barren branches clawed against the stormy sky. The park was filled with clay, the only green from grass tuffs that hung round the base of the trees. About twenty rows of strange plants lined the clay from one end of the park to the other. The heads of these odd flowers were bent over as if sheltering from a driving rain so it was hard to recognise them. They were about the same shape and height as sunflowers but something so happy didn't fit in this landscape.

Derelict houses hovered lonely and grey in the mist just off a potholed road that surrounded the park. Some of the homes

had no windows, others no doors and more still were half built.The wind whistled through the empty shells rattling the steel fencing that lined the roadway.

"It's the Ghost Estate," Boy whispered.

CHAPTER 18

The Ghost Estate

"Ghosts?"

"That's what they say. I heard some men in No Man's Land talk about this place but I thought it was just another story. It's exactly how they described it."

"What is it?" Violet asked.

"I don't really know. I heard them say it's a place of loss and sadness. They said it's where all lonely souls go."

"Go to do what?"

Thunder boomed overhead making Violet jump.

"Can we leave Boy please?" she begged, pulling on his sleeve.

Boy led the way quickly across the park. A sudden movement caught Violet's eye and she stopped.

"Boy look," she shivered, pointing at one of the flowers.

It's petals were closed as if it were asleep. Each petal was delicate, translucent and tiny thread like red veins patterned their surface. She could see right through the petals to the centre of the flower. Something was moving at rapid speed inside. She bent down to investigate when a huge clatter echoed through the empty estate. Boy grabbed her arm and they ran for cover behind the garden wall attached to one of the empty houses.

"I think it's just the steel fencing. The wind must have blown it over," Boy panted, after a few minutes, "Come on let's get out of here."

Violet was about to move when she ducked back down behind the wall pulling Boy with her.

"There's something inside the house" she whispered, "Something moved I swear."

Quickly she crawled across the garden and ducked in under the sill of the main window.

"What are you doing?" Boy whispered, angrily joining her side.

"I'm going to have a look, I have a strange feeling..."

She held onto the edge of the sill and inched herself up to peer through the window. A red bulb hung in the centre of a cement room casting the walls in bloody tones. Rows and rows of small potted plants filled the floor space. The plants were similar to the ones in the park but smaller. Boy tugged on her leg.

"What?"

"Do you see anything?"

"I'm not sure..." she whispered, turning back to the window.

Suddenly she ducked back down.

"What is it Violet? You've gone white!"

"It's...it's..."

"It's what?"

"It's eyes, pots and pots of eyes. They're growing eyes Boy!" she shivered.

Unable to understand, Boy pulled himself up for a look.

"It's eyes," he gasped, falling back down, "It's eyes. Lots and lots of eyes. They were staring at me."

"Those bodies, in the graveyard," Violet trembled, "none of them had eyes."

"But why would anyone want dead peoples eyes Violet? Why would anyone want eyes at all, it's terrible, horrible, I don't even want to think about it!"

They sat under the window ledge in silence. A thought played with Violet but she couldn't grasp it, the Archers, Perfect, the glasses, her Dad...

"My Dad," she said, sitting upright, "my Dad is here Boy. He's here in this place."

"Ssh," Boy whispered, looking anxiously around, "what makes you think that?"

"It's the eyes. The Archers asked him to come and work here because he'd won an award. I remember reading about it in "Eye Spy" I thought it was disgusting. It had something to do with eye transplants."

"But why would the Archers want eye transplants and using the eyes of dead bodies Violet...imagine you'd never be able to see with all the maggots!"

"All I know is that Dad is here. He has to be and we have to rescue him. Please Boy you check that side of the estate and I'll check this one."

"Really...on your own?"

"Yes, I'm not a girl you know!"

"Well you are actually," Boy smiled, then turned and crawled back across the garden.

Violet shivered as he dashed for the other side of the park. She was on her own.

Quickly she crawled across the garden to the next house. Inside there were more rows of eyes. They grew from pulsing veins rooted in pots of dark red clay. The pots bubbled over in blood. Pools of the gruesome liquid seeped across the floor as if a million people were murdered in the room. Small plastic tubes inserted into the side of each pot were connected to a large barrel of blood in the corner, which was feeding the mass of eyes. Her stomach churned as she rested her back against the wall of the house. She was going to vomit. Bile ran up her neck stopping short of her mouth. She steadied then continued her trip across the gardens until she reached the next house. There was another room of eyes but still no Dad.

Suddenly a loud bang shook the estate. Her pulse raced as George Archer strode out from one of the houses across the park towards Boy. All air escaped her lungs. Boy was caught. He had to be. She clambered onto her feet and as quietly as possible followed after the taller twin.

Boy was across the park on his hands and knees looking in another window. George Archer had seen him too.

What could she do? She was powerless. What use would it be if they were both caught? Maybe Boy had to get captured? They might take him to where they were keeping her Dad. She could rescue them both.

George Archer slowed as he reached the wall of the house. Boy was oblivious. Violet wanted to shout but she couldn't. Her friend turned just as George Archer was upon him. The huge man pulled something from his pocket and sprayed Boy in the face. Within seconds he was unconscious. George Archer threw the lifeless body over his shoulder and turned. Violet just managed to hide inside the belly of a rusted old barrel. Moments later, large leather shoes strode past her for the second time that day.

Quickly she crawled out and followed, her legs shaking. She had to be strong. She ducked behind the half built wall of a house and watched as George Archer pushed open the door. When the solid wood slammed firmly shut, Violet jumped to her feet and raced around the back of the house. Double glass doors gave a better view inside, and she watched George Archer carry Boy's lifeless body up the stairs. A few moments later he was back down without her friend, and disappeared out the front door. She raced back round the front to catch his willowy frame return across the green. This was it. Her moment.

CHAPTER 19

The Locked Room

It was clear what she had to do, how to do it was the hard part. First things first, she had to get inside the house.

The windows! The upstairs ones at the back had no glass. Only white plastic sheeting covered the cavities. As quietly as possible she raced around the estate for something that would reach the windows. In the back garden of one of the derelict houses was a battered workbench. Stained coffee and teacups and a half eaten moldy sandwich sat on it's surface as if the place was deserted in a hurry. A sudden chill danced up her spine and her arm hair stood to order. The garden was eerie as though the souls of ghostly builders still worked there. Behind the bench a pile of tools and oddities gathered rust on the dirt. Hidden amongst them was a wooden ladder. Though missing some steps it was long enough to reach the windows.

She picked up the heavy wood and dragged it as quietly as she could to the back garden of Boy's prison. Propping it up against the wall, it fell just a little short of the ledge. With a deep breath she took her first step. The wood cracked under foot so she quickly climbed upwards. Pulling herself over the missing steps she reached the top. The ladder wobbled below as she stretched onto her toes inching her fingers up until they gripped the corner of the ledge. Resting for a minute she then pulled with all her might, wiggled onto the window ledge and tumbled inside, landing with a thump on the cold cement floor.

Thunder boomed loudly above, this time it was followed by a flash of white light that illuminated the empty hallway. It was grey and barren. Shadows haunted every corner. The house was silent. Deadly still.

There were four doors off the hall in front of her and she crawled quickly across the landing to the first. It was empty. Her body alive, she crawled through the darkness to the second. This room was bigger than the last and pitch black. The windows were blocked up with plastic sheeting. Violet felt her way across the floor as another bolt of lighting lit up the place illuminating Boy's lifeless body in the corner.

Her arms weakened as she scurried on all fours towards him. A dog collar was fastened round his neck and secured to the floor by a steel chain. Bruno was etched into a metal tag that hung from the leather, she smiled, the name suited her friend perfectly. The chain was strong, too strong to break and the dog collar was locked shut at the catch. She searched for something to cut through the thick material. Suddenly the front door slammed. She froze. Laughter filled the hallway below. Heavy footsteps walked past the stairs and into a room at the back of the house.

"What do ya suppose he'll do with 'im?" someone snorted.

"Haven't a clue. Probably experiments," another voice laughed.

"Ya reckon? He deserves it anyway. That boy was always a troublemaker. Could never get me hands on 'im in No Mans Land. Slippery little one that."

"Go up and check on him will ya! Make sure he hasn't wriggled out of this one."

Steps pounded towards the stairs. The room was bare, there was nowhere to hide. She scrambled for the door at the other side of the hall and rattled the handle. It was locked. She squealed on reflex.

"Crying like a girl eh Boy!" a voice laughed, nearing the top of the stairs.

Suddenly the door in front of Violet opened. A hand dragged her inside the room just as the Watcher stepped onto the landing. Heavy steps walked down the hall outside as Violet took in her rescuer, a dark haired lady. The woman signalled for Violet to climb into an old wardrobe in the corner of the room. She did as instructed without question or sound.

"I definitely heard a squeal but he's still asleep up here," the Watcher shouted to his friend downstairs.

"How stupid are you ya twit! Go check on your one. Make sure she's not up to no good," roared the reply.

Violet's heart pounded in the darkness as the room door creaked open.

"What are you playing at in here?" the Watcher scowled.

"Cards," the woman coolly replied.

"Mind if I join? Would like to give you a good beatin."

"Of course I mind!"

"Oh ya cheeky," the Watcher said, surging into the room, "I'll smash your pretty little face in two."

"Ah, ah, ah," the woman replied, her voice still even, "do you want me to report you to the Archers?"

"You..." the Watcher growled.

"What," the woman replied, "you think I wouldn't do it?"

134

The door slammed as the Watcher thundered back downstairs.

"One of these days," he roared up from below.

The dark haired lady chuckled.

Violet remained in her hiding place. She wasn't afraid of the woman; she was in awe of her bravery, but for some reason she felt she should wait until asked to leave.

"You can come out now."

Gently she pushed the door of the wardrobe so it swung open gradually revealing the room. The interior was a complete contrast to the rest of the house. It was lit in candles, which cast warm flickers of light and shadow across the ornate wallpaper. The room was full of rich reds and deep woody browns just like the Archer's shop. She stepped out onto the lavish carpet and her feet sunk into it. Beautiful paintings of seascapes and countrysides in gold gilded frames decorated the walls. All of them were wild and full of life like the artists was trying to paint freedom. The room was homely and safe.

"Have a seat young lady," the woman said, gesturing to a chair by an antique wooden table.

The woman was like a Queen or a Princess. Violet climbed the chair, her legs dangled over the ornate edge resting a little from the floor.

"So what brings you here?"

What could she say? She stared blankly at her host. The woman's face was cast in shadow highlighting her delicate features. She was maybe the most beautiful woman Violet had ever seen. She was old though, probably as old as her mother and her hair was long, as long as Violet wished hers to be. It fell down the back of the chair and sat like a jet black veil on the floor. Her face was pale and her large eyes were green, as green as the grass in spring. If ever the word beautiful fit a person, it fitted this woman. Violet wished for a minute she could be just like her.

"Are you okay, has the cat got your tongue young lady?"

"Is there a cat?"

"Oh no it's only an expression," the woman smiled gently.

Violet shifted awkwardly in the chair.

"Are you in trouble?"

Should she tell this woman? She wasn't afraid of her. Could she trust her? She needed a friend.

"Kind of," she answered, "well I'm kind of in trouble but my friend Boy is in big trouble."

"Boy?"

"Yes, I know," Violet smiled, "he's from No Mans Land. He says that's his name."

"Oh! Where is he now?"

"He's next door in the room. He's chained and has a collar on his neck. I'm trying to free him so we can go and find my father."

"Is your father in trouble too?"

"Yes. Well I think so. I think the Archers have him and are making him do some sort of experiments."

The woman's face changed. She turned and walked to the window that overlooked the estate. She didn't speak for a while. Unsure whether to break the silence, Violet distracted herself with the writing desk beside her where there was a letter half written. It wasn't right to read it...

Dear Boys, it started, *this is a day like all the others. I sit in my room and cry for all I have lost...*

"What is your name young lady?" the woman said sharply.

Violet blushed tearing her eyes away from the letter.

"It's...it's Violet," she stuttered.

"That's beautiful. You must have wonderful parents to pick such a beautiful name."

"Em...yes."

Images of her parents flooded her mind. Her throat tightened.

"You know your father is looking for you," the lady said mysteriously.

"Have you seen him?"

Violet sat forward.

"No I'm afraid not Violet but I know what it is like to lose your children and he will not rest until he finds you."

"He didn't lose me. I lost him."

"For a parent it's the same thing Violet. He'll find you."

"Did you find yours?" she asked, then wished she hadn't.

"No," the lady replied.

Silence flooded the room once more.

"I gave up my family a long time ago Violet but I will

always love them. I know when it is my time I will see them again."

"Oh I'm sorry. I didn't mean to be nosy."

"It's okay," the woman smiled, "now don't you want to free your friend? The Watchers will be back soon."

Violet nodded.

"Well then," the woman said.

Walking to the cabinet she pulled a knife from the depths of a drawer.

"Take this, it should cut through the collar."

"Will you come with us?"

"No Violet, but I wish you the best of luck."

"Are you a prisoner?"

"Of sorts."

"But you're not chained?"

"Not physically Violet but the world has changed. There is nothing out there for me now. I am happy here."

"But it's just a room?"

"It's my room Violet," the woman replied abruptly.

"I'm sorry, my Dad would kill me for asking so many questions," Violet said, as she took the knife from the lady and walked to the door, "Thank you."

"Violet, I try not to spend too much time at my window but when I do I notice there is always a lot of activity in that house," she said, pointing across the park, "I think perhaps your father might be there."

"Thank you," Violet said, her body suddenly alive again.

The lady nodded and Violet slipped out the door and back across the hall.

CHAPTER 20

Wickham Terrace

Boy was still unconscious when Violet began to saw through the thick leather. Her progress was slow and he was coming round as she cut.

"Ssh," she whispered, when he started to groan, "It's me. Violet. I'm going to free you. You have to be quiet. There's Watchers downstairs."

Boy slowly opened his eyes and grimaced.

"Do you have to be so rough?" he coughed.

"Do you have to be so ungrateful?"

Chairs scraped across the floor downstairs and Violet increased her pace. Eventually the leather snapped. She helped Boy from the floor. He was a little groggy and wobbled to his feet. They stopped at the corner of the door. Violet checked the hallway.

"Thank you," she whispered across the hall, as they left the room.

"For what?"

"Not you Boy," she replied as they slipped quietly along the dark corridor.

The plastic sheeting blustered in the wind masking any noise as the pair climbed through onto the ledge and down the rickety ladder. Once back on solid ground, Violet pulled Boy round the side of the house and they slid onto their honkers by the pebble dashed wall. They sat in silence catching their breath.

"What happened?" Boy finally whispered.

"George Archer caught you. I saw him but there was nothing I could do. I thought maybe if he caught you he might lead me to Dad."

"So you let him!?"

"Yeah but I rescued you didn't I?" Violet snapped, "and anyway I think my plan might have worked."

"Did you find your Dad?"

"No but I met this woman..."

Violet filled Boy in on all that happened while he slept. When he was up to speed, they decided to cross the estate and have a look at the house the woman had pointed to.

"I have a feeling about it," Violet said, persuading her friend.

Taking care not to be seen the pair ran past the park and crouched down behind the half built wall that surrounded the house. Then, as they had done before, crawled up the clay garden coming to a rest under the main windowsill.

"You have a look," Violet said, her voice shaking.

"You sure?"

She nodded and Boy lifted his head up over the rim of concrete.

"I can't remember what your Dad looks like," he whispered, returning quickly to her side.

"He's tall for a Dad, has reddish brown hair, wears glasses," she said, spurting out words to fill in her father.

"Well in that case I think I saw him," Boy smiled.

"You what...you mean...what do you mean think!?" Violet stammered, quickly peering up over the ledge.

The room beyond the window was different to the others on the estate. Firstly it didn't have rows of planted eyes. Instead it was filled with glass boxes sitting on top of shiny steel tables. Each box held a small red light and under the light rested a solitary eye. There were about six boxes that hugged the edges of the room. In the centre of the space was another table; this one too was shiny steel and filled with piles of papers that streamed onto the floor. A white board crowded with calculations filled the back wall. To the left of it stood a man in a white coat.

"Dad," Violet gasped.

It was him. He'd lost weight; his eyes, underlined by half moon shadows, bulged out from sunken cheeks. He looked sad and lonely. Her Dad had always been strong. Anger filled her bones. She wanted to kill the Archers for what they'd done. She was about to knock on the murky glass when something moved in the corner of the room. She ducked down just as Edward Archer walked past inside.

"Edward Archer! He's in there with my Dad. We have to do something!"

"I don't know Violet," Boy said desperately, "I can't think. It must be the stuff George used to knock me out. My head's cloudy."

"Please Boy. We have to get him out."

"Look, can we get out of here? Just for a bit. If we get some rest we'll be able to think and come up with a plan. If we rush in now we'll get caught."

"No!" Violet snapped a little too loudly.

"Come on. Your Dad's been there a while, a little longer won't do any harm. If we go in without a plan we'll get caught and then who's going to rescue any of us?"

"No Boy. We have to do something now," Violet demanded.

"Violet please be quiet. Edward Archer's just in there."

"You don't want me to get my Dad. That's what wrong with you. Just 'cause you have no parents…"

"What did you say?"

Violet turned her back on her friend. Boy remained under the sill for a minute then without speaking, crawled down the garden and out onto the road. Violet didn't look around. She didn't need Boy. She was fine on her own. Shakily she made her way round the side of the house.

It was weird without him, scarier, but she had to forget her fear. Her Dad needed her. She walked to the back garden and looked at the windows. They all had glass, that plan was a no go. She tiptoed to the other side of the house. There was a narrow pathway separating this home from its neighbours.

145

The path was pitch black. She felt her way by the wall and about halfway down she came across a door. There was a faint sound over her shoulder. She looked round but couldn't see anything in the darkness. She was about to grab the handle when she froze. The hair on the back of her neck stood up.

"Well look what I caught," a Watcher whispered into her ear.

Violet turned quickly, her heart pounding. His arms rested either side of the doorway blocking her escape. She tried to dash under one but the Watcher was too quick and grabbed her shirt pulling her out onto the path.

"Well won't I be Mr. Edward's favourite," he laughed, shining a torch directly into her eyes.

She kicked and wriggled but couldn't get free.

"DUCK" somebody suddenly yelled.

It was Boy. Violet quickly ducked down as a large rock whizzed past landing smack on the bridge of the Watcher's nose. He fell to the ground roaring in pain. Boy grabbed Violet's hand and they raced down the front garden.

As they reached the park Watchers were emerging from everywhere to give chase. The pair were sprinting through the

146

sleeping plants when Violet tumbled roughly to the ground. One of the creatures had wrapped itself round her leg. Boy tried to pull his friend free but the eyeball wouldn't let go. The Watchers were almost upon them when he grabbed the stem and ripped. Blood gushed out from the severed vein in all directions. Quickly Boy shoved the plant into his pocket and helped Violet from the grass.

Suddenly a terrifying noise cut through the night like a thousand wailing cats. The once sleeping flowers pulled back their petals and shrieked into the mist. Shaking in a manic frenzy they threw themselves at Boy and Violet as they raced past. Barely escaping the park, the pair dashed by a large billboard of a happy family marking the entrance to the Ghost Estate. They were now in a world of narrow streets, the Watchers just behind.

"Where are we?" Violet panted.

"We're in No Mans Land," Boy said, as they raced down a laneway, "it's the furthest edges."

"Do you know where you're going?" Violet asked breathless as they shot down another alley, the Watchers still on their tail.

"No!"

Suddenly she caught sight of a street sign. *Wickham Terrace*; she knew the name but from where?

"Down here," she said.

The Watchers feet pounded just behind the last bend. There was an old shop sign hanging out on the street: "Prescription Optical Makers."

"In here," Violet said, forcing open the door.

They closed it gently and rested with their backs to the worn wood as the Watchers darted by outside oblivious to their hiding place.

"Where are we?" Boy whispered.

"I'm not sure," Violet shrugged, just as a light lit up the shop.

"Who goes there?" someone said from the shadows.

"We don't mean you any harm," Violet insisted, "we were being chased and…"

"Where did you get those?" the man croaked, his voice was dusty as if it hadn't been used in while.

Violet looked at Boy who shrugged.

"Answer me!" the man snapped.

"Where did I get what?" Violet replied, her voice now shaky too.

"Your glasses, where did you get them?"

"I found them."

"Don't lie to me girl. Where did you get them?"

"I found them, I promise. They were under my mattress. Here you can have them," she said, taking the frames from her face and walking with her arm outstretched.

The man moved forward and grabbed the glasses from her grasp.

"How did they get under your mattress?" he said, stepping out from the shadows, "I think you're telling fibs little girl. The last time I saw these they were in the hands of my brother."

"You're...you're...you're William Archer," Violet stammered.

Boy looked at his friend as if she had ten heads.

"And you are?" the man continued.

"Violet, Violet Brown," she stuttered, "and this is my friend Boy."

CHAPTER 21

William Archer

William Archer was a tall man though not as tall as George, he was also a wide man though not as wide as Edward and this combination meant he was completely in proportion. He was unkempt, dirty and looked like he'd spent a thousand years in his clothes. His hair was long and streaked in tones of grey. His beard was long too and he wore both beard and hair wrapped like a scarf round his neck. He had a kind face and as he emerged from the shadows it was almost impossible not to stare at his eyes. One was dark almost black while the other was a cold blue like an icy winter's morning. Violet's Dad had told her that some people were born with different coloured eyes but William was the first one she'd met.

A cluttered table rested by the front window and William cleared it off before calling over the pair. Violet sat down on one side and Boy on the other. The window was caked in dirt, which was safer, surely the Watchers couldn't see in.

"Excuse the mess," William Archer coughed, "I haven't had guests in a while".

"It's fine," Violet replied in her polite voice, "it's just like my room."

William smiled uncomfortably, he didn't seem used to the company of children or maybe it was the company of anyone at all.

"Have you lived here long?" Violet asked, breaking an awkward silence.

Boy stared in shock at his friend and frantically gestured towards the door.

"It's okay Boy. He's not like his brothers."

Her friend's eyes fell towards the table avoiding William and his cheeks reddened in embarrassment.

"And how do you know I'm not like my brothers?" William asked, a hint of a smile in his voice.

"Because I saw your message under my desk at school and because I met your Mam. She said you were a good son."

"She did?" William said, his eyes glassing over, "how is Iris, is she well?"

"I think so, I only met her for a minute though."

"I've been here so long," William whispered, as if to himself, "I'm not sure I remember what she looks like anymore."

"Everyone remembers what their Mam looks like no matter how long they've been away. She's your Mam," Violet replied.

She glanced across at Boy then quickly down at her hands avoiding his eyes.

"You're a wise one for someone your age!" William Archer laughed.

The gentle sound filled the faded shop and Violet knew immediately, though she'd kind of known it already, that she liked William Archer. Boy seemed to know it too. His stiff upright posture softened with the laughter.

"So," William said running his fingers over the frames in his hands, "how did you find my glasses?"

"Oh," Violet shouted suddenly jumping up, "I'm not wearing any glasses! I can see! I'm not blind!"

William laughed again, this time his laughter was big and full and it seemed to shake the shop. The deep-bellied sound was infectious and suddenly Boy and Violet found themselves laughing too.

"So you're from Perfect," he smiled, regaining a little control.

"No I'm not!" Violet snapped, "I lived there for a bit but I'm not from there."

"She's from there," Boy teased, "I'm not though, I'm from here."

Violet shot Boy a dirty look.

"Maybe you're not from there but you've lived there. You must have, why else would you be blind?" William continued.

"But I'm not blind," Violet said, "that's what I'm trying to say."

"I know Violet but I'll let you in on a secret. You never were blind. They just made you believe you were."

"Who?" Violet and Boy replied in unison.

"My brothers. They made everyone in Perfect blind."

"Why?"

"It's a long story Violet," William continued, "and you still haven't told me how you came across my glasses?"

"I didn't know they were yours but I found them under

my bed. I'm telling the truth."

"Well how did they get there?" William said, his voice still disbelieving.

"She did," Boy interrupted, "I mean she did find them under her bed."

"Ah," William smiled, "I thought it might have something to do with you. All the children in No Mans Land have nifty fingers."

"I didn't steal them if that's what you're saying," Boy replied angrily, "I just had them."

Violet stared blankly at friend.

"But I thought my Dad…"

"I know what you thought," Boy sighed, "that's why I didn't tell you. I didn't mind what you thought as long as you could see me. I'm sorry Violet it's just I was sick of being invisible and you looked like good fun."

"It's okay Boy," Violet smiled, "I'm happy you gave them to me."

"You still haven't answered my question," William Archer said, staring at Boy.

"I swear I didn't steal them. I just always had them, since I was born. In the orphanage they said I was born wearing them and I believed it for years, then one of the nurses told me that the glasses were hidden in my blankets the day I arrived."

"Oh."

William fell into a deep silence. Boy and Violet communicated in stolen glances across the table afraid to break the quiet.

"And they, the nurses, did they say anything else?"

"No."

Boy was silent now too. His head dropped and his hand slipped down off the table. He began to fumble with something in his pocket.

"There is one thing," he mumbled, "this was left with them. I like to think it's from my mother..."

He pulled a note from his pocket and unfolded it. Catching Violet's shocked expression he blushed a rosy red. He passed it to William. The note once white was now grey, crumpled and worn, like paper long ripped from a copybook. Violet watched Boy closely as William Archer read. Then he folded it and without a word handed the note back to her friend.

"Can I read it?" she asked, almost leaping across the table.

Slowly Boy passed it over and Violet opened the note. She imagined Boy's mother scribbling the mysterious message.

So you will never be invisible.

Something about it felt oddly familiar. Gently she folded the precious paper and handed it back to her friend.

"It's beautiful Boy."

He smiled, looked at it once more, then carefully put it back in his pocket.

"Does it mean anything to you Mr. Archer?" Violet asked.

"Em...no, no Violet it doesn't," William Archer said, rising from the table, "Now I'm being a terrible host. Would you like some tea? I could do with a cup after all the excitement of the day."

"Yes please," Violet smiled, "do you have any of the stuff from Perfect. It's my favourite."

"No Violet just normal tea here I'm afraid."

William Archer left the pair at his table and walked back into the shadows of the room.

"Where do you think he's gone?" Boy whispered.

"I suppose the kitchen," Violet teased.

"Violet after all that's happened you're still a little stupid. Do you really trust him? He's an Archer. I think we should leave."

"No Boy, he's good I can tell. Just give him a chance. Anyway why would somebody evil invent glasses so the people in No Mans Land could be seen again? Surely if he was like his brothers he wouldn't do that- and what about the most obvious thing?" Violet whispered, leaning further across the table, "He lives here, in No Mans Land. Who'd choose that?"

"Thanks," Boy huffed.

"Well you didn't choose it, your mother did and she must have had her reasons. I think she was a good person even though she gave you up."

"What do you mean?"

"Well I mean your Mam; she must have known what was going on. If I had a kid I wouldn't like it to grow up in Perfect. I'd choose No Mans Land too but only if I knew what was happening in Perfect, most people are blind to it. And she left you the glasses. She wanted you to know what was happening too. I think she wanted you to do something about it. If she couldn't maybe she thought her son could. Don't you think?"

"I never really thought about it. Anyway who even knows if it was my Mam. It could have been anyone. Like I said I have no parents. You have some imagination Violet. All that from one sentence."

Boy sneered his friend just as William Archer walked back into the room with a tray of chipped mugs and a handle-less jug of milk.

"THE TEA!" Violet shouted, jumping up and almost knocking the tray from William's hands, "It has to be the tea!"

"Yes it's tea Violet," Boy smirked, "you really are a bit crazy sometimes."

"No Boy, don't you see it has to be the tea. I never drank tea before I got to Perfect. Then the first night we arrived the Archers were there and they had tea ready. They told us everyone drinks it in Perfect and when I tried it I knew why. It tasted like anything I wanted it to taste like, an ice cream Sunday, fizzy cola bottles, apple drops, anything. I had two cups that night and the next day we were all blind. I never thought... Everybody drinks it! Even in school we had tea breaks all the time. And now I haven't had it for a few days and I can see again. It can't be by accident."

"My brothers must have gotten better," William sighed leaving down the tray, "in my day they were using tablets. They prescribed them to everyone for all sorts of eye ailments. It didn't matter. They even dropped them in people's drinks when they weren't looking. It was a messy business."

"Why didn't you stop them?" Violet asked.

"Well for a while I did and I had a bit of a gang behind me. Soon people started to change. The town began to look perfect to them and they stopped listening. Then the Watchers came onboard. They were just a gang of thugs my brothers drafted in and paid for their dirty deeds. One day, they caught hold of me and I ended up here. I set up my shop and started work on reversing the effect of the glasses. That's when I made these," he said, picking the frames from the table.

"How did your brothers get them?" Boy asked.

"They caught me," William said, looking at his hands, "I'd gone into town with the glasses; I was hoping that if my mother or Macula could just put them on they would know I hadn't left them. They'd know I hadn't gone away."

"Who's Macula?" Violet asked.

"Just someone I knew once."

William moved his hands in front of his face to shield his eyes. Quickly he wiped them and began to pour the tea, handing a cup to each of his visitors.

"I'm okay thanks," Boy said, holding up his hands.

"It's safe," William smiled, "I'm not like them. I'll never be like them."

His tone was firm and Boy took the cup from him. Violet looked over at her friend then took the first sip.

CHAPTER 22

The Reimaginator

"I think I have an idea," Violet said, placing down her cup.

"Oh no! Not another one," Boy teased, "the last idea ended with the Watchers trying to kill us!"

"Ha ha, very funny Boy! Anyway," she said, looking at William who appeared lost in thought, "if it's the tea that makes everyone blind then we get rid of the tea! Soon the whole of Perfect will be able to see again. Don't you think Mr. Archer...Mr. Archer?"

"Oh yes, sorry Violet what were you saying?"

"The tea, if we get rid of the tea then everyone will be able to see again."

"I'm not sure it's so simple Violet. The glasses my brothers use don't just block a person's vision to certain things. They also suck out the imagination. At least they did in my day. At night the Watchers sneak into people homes, put their glasses into a special machine, I call it the 'Super Sucker.' The machine sucks out the imagination and the Watchers bring it back to my brothers shop to be stored."

"That's what we saw in the Archers shop Violet. All those jars of colour. They must have been imaginations!" Boy said, getting excited.

"But why?" Violet asked William Archer ignoring Boy's enthusiasm.

"Oh it's simple really. People are much easier to control when they have no imagination. They don't ask questions and believe anything you tell them. Simple fact is a human isn't much at all when they lack imagination."

"But what about me? Why didn't the glasses work on me?" Violet asked.

"Well I'm not sure but I do have a theory. It happens sometimes, my brothers just can't control some people no matter how much they try. Those people always end up here in No Mans Land. I imagine given a little more time you would have been thrown here too. Needless to say they would have told your family some story or other and they would accept it..."

"Like they did with Dad," Violet interrupted, "the Archers told Mam he'd gone away on business and she believed them. Dad would never do that without telling us."

"Exactly Violet, your mother is a Perfect citizen so to speak."

"But I still don't understand, why didn't it work on me?" she said again.

"Well I believe some people just have too much."

"Too much what?" Boy asked.

"Too much imagination. They either have vast stores or they can regenerate it. I'm not sure which. The majority of people just have a set amount and when it's gone, it's gone."

"Bet I have more than you Boy," Violet smiled, proudly.

"I suppose you are a freak," he laughed.

"My studies have shown it could be genetic." William continued, "You said your father was also taken to No Mans Land Violet- which proves my point."

"No I didn't," Violet replied, "they took my Dad to the Ghost Estate. We were just there. He's a prisoner and the Archers are forcing him to carry out experiments. They're growing eyes but we don't know why."

"Growing what?" William coughed, spitting out some of his tea.

"Eyes," Boy replied, "just like this one."

Boy pulled the half dead plant from his pocket leaving it down in front of William Archer. The creature wriggled and squirmed for a moment then stopped. A clump of congealed blood spewed out onto the table from it's severed vein. The eye looked from Violet to William finally resting on Boy then shuddered once more and died.

William's face lost all colour as he took up a pencil and poked the specimen.

"Did you really..." he stopped mid sentence and rose quickly to look out the window.

"You two into the back now," he said urgently, "Follow down that way there's a door. Go through it and wait until I come get you."

He was stiff and stern; William Archer had suddenly come alive.

"What is it, what's wrong?" Violet said.

"The Watchers, they're searching the street, probably looking for you two. I'll try get rid of them."

Violet and Boy did as they were told and slipped into the shadows in the direction William Archer pointed. The place was pitch black and they had to put their arms out so as not to bump into anything. Boy hit the door first and grunted.

"Not a sound!" William barked, across the room.

Searching in the darkness, Violet found the handle and turned it as quietly as possible. Taking care not to utter a sound, the pair slipped in through the door closing it silently behind them.

They were standing in an office of sorts. Judging by the mess it was definitely a man's office. A single bulb, dirty with dust, clung to a wire in the middle of the room casting a faint yellow glow around the space. There was a table by the far wall overflowing in loose papers and piles of notebooks. They were also covered in dust as if they hadn't been looked at in a very long time. Violet had just picked a notebook from the pile when Boy called her.

"Come here," he said, his ear stuck to the door, "Listen."

She took a space next to Boys.

"They ran past about half an hour ago," a voice growled.

"Well as I said I haven't seen them. I've been shut up in my office all day."

"Working on your experiments I suppose," one of the Watchers laughed.

"I gave that up years ago boys you know that. Happy to tow the line these days."

"That's what you say alright. So you don't mind if we come in for a look then?"

Violet's eyes widened. Quickly the pair scurried around the room for somewhere to hide. In her haste Violet tripped over a solid lump in the carpet. She bent down to inspect the threadbare rug. There was something underneath. She pulled it back to reveal a trap door.

"Boy, quickly," she whispered, heaving at the solid block of wood.

Within seconds he was at her side and had yanked open the door. A ladder reached up from the darkness below. Violet quickly descended. Boy followed pulling the carpet back on top of the trap door before closing it above him. They held their silence as footsteps entered the room above.

"Do you think they heard us?" Violet whispered.

"No I don't think so," Boy replied, breathless.

Something brushed off Violet's ear and she jumped. It was like a piece of string, she reached for it in the darkness and pulled. There was a quick click, a small sizzle and suddenly the room flooded with light. The place looked like the inside of her cousin's hay barn. The walls were made from stones of all different shapes and sizes mixed with thick beams of dark brown wood. Thinner wooden beams striped the ceiling and the floor was slabbed in even more stone.

Sheets and sheets of paper covered the walls. They were mainly drawings of glasses with arrows running from one picture to another. Hand scribbled notes covered the drawings. Some of the writing was small and in black while other words were large, in red and looked very important. William Archer had been experimenting with different ways to make his own glasses. All the notes were dated and the most recent was about ten years old. He also had lots of notes on the imagination, his theories worked out across the yellowing pages. There was a diagram titled the "Reimaginator". It was a strange contraption made up mainly of what looked like lots of bagpipes. There were dials and buttons sticking out all over the odd looking machine.

"Violet," Boy whispered.

Engrossed in the "Reimaginator" she ignored her friend.

"Violet," he said this time a little louder.

Still there was no response.

"Violet you have to see this!"

"What Boy!" she snapped, turning around.

Violet gasped. Boy was standing in front of a crooked wooden table on top of which sat the "Reimaginator". It was exactly like the drawing. Lots of pipes snaked round the machine off in different directions; each pipe was connected to a leather bag. Seven leather bags like giant lungs stuck out from the side of the machine. A gold-framed glass cabinet sat in the middle of the "Reimaginator". It was empty at the moment but in the drawing it was full with coloured gas.

"What is it?" Boy whispered.

"I think it gives people back their imagination," Violet slowly replied.

Suddenly something shuffled above. Boy dived for the light plunging the place back into darkness.

CHAPTER 23

Welcome to Adequate

"I see you found my den,"

William Archer peered down from the trap door.

"Yes," Violet replied, "It's amazing."

"Oh it was all a long time ago," William said, brushing off the compliment, "Now come on you better get out of here. It took a lot of persuading to get rid of those Watchers and I am sure they'll be back."

Violet and Boy did what they were told and climbed out of the basement.

"How did you get rid of them?" Violet asked, when she was back in the room.

"Oh years of compliance," William smiled half-heartedly; "If it had happened ten years ago they would never have believed me."

"Why?"

"Well I didn't exactly tow the line when I first came here as you can see from my experiments," he laughed remembering, "but I've been a good boy since. You might even call me perfect."

"Why did you stop?" Violet asked.

Boy gave her a warning look.

"There was no reason left to fight," William replied, closing the trap door and replacing the carpet. "Now you two better go. I don't want to get into any trouble."

"But please," Violet said, "you could help. I saw the "Reimaginator". We could fix Perfect."

"Violet," Boy warned.

"Please," Violet said again, "Please Mr. Archer, I know we could do it. Now that we know about the tea and we have your invention and all your research. I know we could save Perfect. We could save my family."

"Violet let's go," Boy said, pulling her away.

"Please Mr. Archer?"

"Enough Violet!" William snapped, "Perfect is fine as it is. I gave all that up long ago and I'm happier for it. I am sorry about your father but I am afraid I can't help. You will have to suffer the faith of the rest of us and get used to No Mans Land. The quicker you do that, the better for you."

"But you can help I know you can. I know you're not happy."

"Violet. You've gone too far now. You don't know me. Now please both of you leave. I have helped you enough."

He herded the pair across his shop and out the door leaving them alone in the laneway. Violet was devastated. William Archer was meant to be nice, he was meant to be different.

It was now late morning and though they were both tired they had to spend the rest of the day hiding from the Watchers in No Mans Land. Boy knew a lot of secret places and they avoided danger sometimes only by the narrowest of margins. As darkness set in, both exhausted, Boy led the way in silence through the streets coming to a stop outside a stark grey building.

"We're here," he said, "you can stay for the night and tomorrow we'll figure out what to do."

"Where are we?" Violet asked.

"My home," Boy smiled, "It's the orphanage. I'll sneak

you in and you can sleep in the playroom. It's better we don't tell anyone yet just in case the Watchers are still looking for you. After a few days, when it's all blown over, I'll tell the nurses. They're used to kids turning up from Perfect so I'm sure they'll give you a bed."

"But I don't want to live here Boy," Violet panicked, "I live with my parents. I want to go home!"

"Ssh Violet please," Boy said, hugging his friend, "we'll figure something out. Tonight anyway you'll stay here."

He led her in through gigantic wrought iron gates that dwarfed the pair. There were grand carved double doors round the side of the imposing building and Boy gently pushed them open. Checking the coast was clear; he tiptoed down the enormous hallway through another set of double doors.

"In here," he whispered, his voice echoed in the space.

Violet followed. The room on the other side was sparse and cold, the ceiling stretched right to the sky. The walls were covered in plain white wallpaper, which was torn away in places revealing years of chipped paint. A rickety bookcase holding a tiny collection of aging books and a small box of broken and tattered toys rested in one corner. Violet was overwhelmed, the room was huge and lonely not like her home where she was safe and loved.

Boy left to get some blankets. Seeking out a small space Violet crouched onto her honkers and nestled down deep into the far corner of the room. She was wrong. She wasn't safe at home anymore. She wasn't loved either. Tears watered her vision and Boy was a blur as he tiptoed back into the room.

"Violet," he whispered.

"Over here Boy."

"What are you doing here?" he laughed, finding her curled up in the corner.

"I don't know," she half smiled, "it felt safer."

"Don't worry. They don't let us play in here much, so you won't be disturbed. I'll come down early in the morning to get you up. Take these."

He handed her a worn old duvet and pillow. He also had a cup of hot water and an apple in his hand and he left them on the floor beside her.

"Are these yours?" she asked.

"I'll be fine," he replied, "I never get cold anyway."

"No, I can't," Violet insisted, handing back the blankets.

"I'm a boy," he laughed, running over to the door, "unlike girls I'm tough, I can take the cold."

Violet smiled as her friend snuck quietly out of the room. Even though she pretended she didn't; she secretly liked his teasing.

Spreading the duvet out on the floor she lay on top, grabbed the corner and rolled, wrapping it tight around her narrow figure. Making sure there were no air holes, she pulled the pillow into place and fell asleep exhausted.

The morning sun warmed her cheek pulling Violet from a restful sleep. There wasn't a sound in the huge house so it must have been early. She lay listening to the dawn chorus as her breath formed circles in the space above her head. Bored she scanned the room.

There was a small bookshelf in the corner. On the count of three she raced across the freezing tiles, grabbed a book and sprinted back to the warmth of her blankets. The book was old and worn, tattered round the edges. *A History of Adequate* it was called and a picture of what looked like the main street in Perfect sat on the cover. Biting into her apple, Violet opened the book.

Welcome to Adequate, our perfect little town.

She flicked through the pages. Adequate was definitely Perfect. The streets, the shops even some the faces were the same except for one thing. Nothing looked perfect in Adequate. Adequate wasn't glossy, it was nice, even lovely but some of the flowerpots were cracked, paint was chipped here and there and the people looked normal, good normal, not shiny at all.

She flicked onto a picture and her heart stopped. It was a wedding scene. A beautiful couple stood centre, behind them was the square in Perfect and either side their families. The caption read "Macula Lashes and William Archer, son of Iris and the late Arnold Archer residents of Adequate, surrounded by family on their wedding day."

"Boo!"

Violet leapt from her bed.

"It's only me Violet," Boy laughed, "can't believe I scared ya. Hey, I didn't know you could read!?"

"Boy," Violet snapped, catching her breath, "what if I'd screamed or something."

"Your face was hilarious," Boy laughed.

Violet forced a smile and sat back down on the duvet.

"You have to see this," she said, "I think I know how we'll get William to help us."

"No Violet," Boy said, quickly becoming serious, "he doesn't want to. You can't force him. We'll find another way."

"But I know he'll want to Boy. I'm telling you," Violet said, pushing the book under his nose.

"Oh, it's him, William," Boy said, rubbing the picture, "He's getting married? He looks much younger. And there's George and Edward, they don't look too happy."

"Where? I didn't see them. Anyway, it's not them I'm on about, it's her," Violet said, pointing to William's bride.

"What about her?"

"Well I met her."

"What do you mean you met her?"

"When you were in the house and I rescued you…"

"I rescued you too you know."

"It's not a competition Boy. Anyway when I rescued you, she was the woman in the room across the hall."

"Really? You sure? What would she be doing there if she's William's wife?"

"Well how do I know but it was definitely her. Maybe the Archers kidnapped her. William said they took everything from him and that's why he won't fight. Maybe she's everything they took."

"That still doesn't mean he'll help us."

"Well he'll have to 'cause I'm sure he wants to rescue her and we're the only people who know where she is."

"Violet that's blackmail," Boy whispered, "you can't do that."

"I know," she smiled, "I wouldn't anyway, but I have a feeling he'll help us. I think he really wants to. He just needs a little push to get brave again."

"'Get brave again?" Boy laughed, "That's a great way of putting it. I think you need to get a little unbrave again. Where's the crying Violet gone, the girly girl one?"

Violet elbowed Boy sharply in the ribs then climbed up from the floor.

"Come on Boy. Let's get William brave again!"

CHAPTER 24

The Persuasion

"Not you two again," William Archer sighed, as he opened his door a crack.

"Please Mr. Archer can we come in?" Violet asked, "I have something I need to tell you."

"Violet I told you yesterday I am not interested in helping you. Now please leave me a…"

"It's about Macula."

William's face changed. He glanced down the street in both directions then quickly ushered the pair inside. Closing the door, he paused against the wood then turned to face them.

"What do you know about Macula?" he asked, his tone firm, "this better be good children because you have worn my patience thin."

Violet looked at Boy then pulled the book from under her jumper.

"I found this," she said, handing it over, "I've marked the page."

William took the book, walked to the table and sat down. His body slackened as he opened it at the mark. Unconsciously, he thumbed the paper.

"You looked beautiful that day," he whispered.

Violet walked over to the table and sat down. Boy followed her lead.

"I found it in the orphanage," she said "is Adequate now Perfect?"

William nodded.

"When did it change?" Boy asked.

"A long time ago," William sighed, lifting his head from the page for the first time, "You see Adequate was a lovely town. It had its good and bad points but on the whole it was a happy place. Balanced."

"So what happened to it?" Violet asked.

"My brothers," William replied, his anger visible, "they were always too big for their boots you see. They were perfect in school and perfect at home but they didn't get the praise they thought they deserved. I wasn't perfect, I was a bit of a joker but I was popular. I had loads of friends. I was also my mother's pet."

"Iris?" Violet interrupted.

William nodded "I wasn't perfect and still you see I was popular. That killed my brothers. It ate away at their perfect theories. They hated me. It hurt for a while but I got used to it, that was until the day Macula arrived."

"She was beautiful," Violet said, looking at the picture.

"She turned up in our town like an exotic bird. We fell for her immediately. All of us did. Every young man in Adequate was in love with Macula Lashes. My brothers tried everything possible to win her heart. George sent her flowers, Edward wrote her poems but nothing worked. I did nothing. I was too shy and never thought she'd like me. The strange thing was doing nothing seemed to work. That's women for you," William smiled at Boy who blushed.

"We fell in love and it broke my brothers' hearts'. From that moment on they plotted ways to get rid of me and anything else that didn't fit into their vision of a perfect world. That's how "Adequate" came to be "Perfect". They blinded the population, invented their glasses and threw anyone who didn't conform into No Mans Land, a place where their glasses couldn't penetrate. They made us invisible. I've been here ever since. They told my mother and Macula that I'd left them. They took my life from me."

"That's terrible," Violet said, as the old man walked over to a cabinet by the wall.

"This is her," he said, pulling a picture from the drawer and joining them back at the table.

"Wow," Boy smiled, staring at the picture, "I can see why everyone fancied her."

"She really is beautiful," Violet added.

"Was beautiful," William said, his voice barely audible, "she left Perfect. Met another man George told me. They were both killed on honeymoon when their hot air balloon fell from a height to the ground."

"Oh," Violet laughed.

William looked up from the picture.

"Do you find death funny?" he snapped.

"No just George's story. I didn't know he had any imagination. Except when it's in a jar," Violet smiled.

181

"Violet are you sure?" Boy hissed across the table, "I really don't know about this."

"About what?"

"Well," Violet said, "I don't think Macula was in a hot air balloon or with another man or had even forgotten about you for a second."

"What do you mean?" William said pushing back from the table.

"I met her," Violet smiled, "I met her only a few days ago in the Ghost Estate."

William looked at Violet then strode to the cabinet and gently put the picture back in it's place. Without a word he walked into the shadows and through the door to his office.

"I knew we shouldn't have come Violet," Boy whispered, leaning across the table, "Let's go please. I don't think he's too happy with us."

She was about to answer when a door banged loudly and William Archer emerged back through the shadows. He stopped short of the table and flung something down onto the wood. A gold ring wobbled and rolled before falling over dead.

"Her wedding ring," he snapped, "Now please leave this

house. I have lost all but a morsel of my patience."

Violet picked up the delicate golden ring and stared at the inscription written in swirly letters.

> To my love, everything is clear when I'm with you.
> William.

"But..." she said, before losing her words.

Boy got up from his seat and grabbed Violet's hand.

> "Come on," he said, pulling her from the chair, "we have to go. I'm sorry Mr. Archer. We didn't mean..."

> "Her eyes," Violet said suddenly, "her eyes are green. As green as the grass in spring."

William Archer walked to the door, grabbed the handle and wrenched it open.

> "And she mentioned a son," Violet stammered, as Boy pulled her through the doorway, " she said she knew what it was like to lose a child. She said the Archers had taken everything from her and the world meant nothing now."

The door slammed behind them and Violet and Boy were left alone in the narrow back lane of No Mans Land.

"It was her. I swear Boy," Violet sobbed, as they reached the corner.

Suddenly another bang shook the street. The pair turned to see William Archer standing outside his house.

"Tell me again what she said Violet?" he shouted.

Violet looked at Boy who pushed her towards William.

"Tell him," he whispered.

"What did she say Violet?" the man asked again.

"Em... she said the Archers took everything from her. She said she had nothing to live for."

"Before that."

"She said she knew what it was like to lose a child and that my Dad would never stop looking for me."

"You better come back in," William said, returning to the house.

Violet looked at Boy who had rejoined her side and they walked back up the street together. William Archer was sitting in his chair by the window and the pair took their spots at the table. For a while there was silence. William swirled the gold wedding ring round his little finger.

"We had a child," he said, without looking up, "We called him Alfred. Macula said it was a proud name, one she knew he would wear well. I didn't argue I loved her too much for that. Alfred was the most beautiful child I'd ever seen, he took after his mother. He was five when he died."

Tears formed and William stopped speaking. Violet glanced at Boy who looked as shocked as she felt. She was about to speak when her friend shook his head and she stopped. After a few moments William continued.

"I had been away trying to rally up support against my brothers. It was a crazy crusade Macula said and it was one she disagreed with. My brothers called round while I was out and Macula got into an argument with them. They were trying to persuade her against me. No one noticed the door was open. My mother was the first to spot it and she chased out of the house after Alfred but by then it was too late. He'd fallen under the wheels of a passing car. It was torture. No Mans Land is not a patch on the grief of losing a child. Macula always said the Archers took her son, I never knew if she included me in that but if so she had every right. I should have been there."

"I'm sorry," Boy said, "we shouldn't have come."

185

"No Boy. I am the one who is sorry. It's just I haven't spoken about Alfred in a long time. It's easier than it used to be," he smiled.

"How long ago was the accident?" Violet asked.

"A long time ago Violet, a few years before Perfect. We got through it but I continued to try and convince people of what was going on. My work became my life. I wanted to forget about my son and my wife suffered. She said that treacherous day she lost everything to the Archers. That's how I knew you had met her. How is she?" William asked, his eyes glassy.

"She's good," Violet replied, "she helped me. She saved me from the Watchers. I asked her if she wanted to escape and that is when she said all that stuff about having nothing left. I think she was scared."

"Did she mention me?"

"No I didn't ask her many questions."

"Oh," William sighed, "I expect that was for the best. Did she seem well though? Healthy? At least a little happy?"

"She seemed healthy," Violet said, "but I don't think she was happy."

William stood up from the table and paced the room. The sadness left his face. His mouth narrowed and his eyes darted from side to side, he was concentrating, thinking. He marched towards the table. His hand held firm in a fist, which he slammed ferociously onto the solid wood. Everything jumped including Violet and Boy.

"Those blasted brothers," he snarled, "They have made their last pair of spectacles."

Violet smiled at Boy then up at William Archer.

"I told Boy all we had to do was make you brave again."

"I'm feeling a lot braver thank you Violet."

CHAPTER 25

Time For Tactics

William Archer walked to the cabinet and pulled out a notepad and pencil.

"Now tell me everything you know. I need all the details," he said, rejoining the pair at the table.

Violet and Boy told their tale with enthusiasm. Starting when Violet put on William's glasses, to the Archer's shop, the Ghost Estate, the eyes, Macula and finding Violet's Dad. William Archer interjected with questions. He pushed them to remember details and when they'd finished Violet and Boy were exhausted.

"I've never had to think this hard about anything," Boy yawned, rubbing his forehead.

"We have to get everything down Boy. My brothers are formidable opponents and we can't go into battle ill prepared."

"We're going into battle?" Violet said her eyes large.

"We're not going to kill anybody are we?" Boy asked.

"No Boy," William smiled, "we're going to cause mayhem and madness. My brothers won't know what hit them. I've been waiting for things to happen a very long time and you two have made me see sense. I can't sit down and wait any longer, I have to make them happen. Waiting is a coward's game. I have to fight for what I want."

"Well I want my family back," Violet said.

"As do I Violet," William replied.

Boy sat silently fidgeting opposite them. Violet flushed, he had no family.

"Boy imagine: you'll be free of me," she smiled.

He smiled back but it didn't reach his eyes.

"Now," William said, pushing up from the table, "can you two draw a map of the Ghost Estate. It needs to be as accurate as possible. Mark down the house you think Macula is in and where all the Watchers are stationed..."

"And where my Dad is," Violet interrupted.

"Of course Violet," William Archer said, quickly walking back into the shadows of the room.

Violet and Boy were arguing over the number of houses in the estate when William rejoined them at the table. He was laden down with bits and bobs of equipment, reams of paper and a jar of gooey water in which the dead eye plant was suspended.

"Eeeeuh!" Violet said, as the jar was placed in front of her, "that thing is disgusting."

"I did a little investigation after you left. It brought me back to the old days" William smiled, as he picked up the eyeball, "I discovered what my brothers are up to with these little beauties."

He handed the plant to Violet and then Boy pointing out an incision he'd made in the centre of the eye.

"See this," he said, gently lifting a thin layer of rose coloured film from the pupil, "this is made from the same material as the lenses in their glasses. I remember my brothers' main frustration with Perfect was that is wasn't quiet Perfect, not when everyone in the town wore glasses. With these new eyes that problem is solved. Genius; in a twisted kind of way."

"You mean they were going to take out people's eyes and give them new ones?" Boy said, paling round the cheeks.

"Exactly Boy," William smiled, "I don't expect my brothers would explain it that way though. I'm sure they'd say it was laser surgery or something of that sort. I've heard that's all the rage in the world of optometry these days."

"But what about the imaginations?" Violet asked, "how would they steal them then?"

"Oh Violet," William smiled, "No matter what I say about my brothers I have to give them one thing. They are extremely clever. I'm sure people must have a number of check ups after laser surgery, don't you think? Three or four sessions should be sufficient to steal a whole imagination these days."

"Oh," Violet gasped, "we have to stop them. If they swap people's eyes there'll be no hope of them ever changing back."

"Exactly Violet and that's why we have to act quickly."

"What are you planning?" Boy asked.

"I propose a full on assault. Storm the estate. Rescue Macula...and Violet's Dad of course and destroy the eyes."

Violet was looking at William's scribbled notes when she caught Boy making signals at the other side of the table.

"What's wrong?" she mimed.

William Archer pulled his head from his papers.

"Is everything alright?"

"There's something wrong with Boy," Violet said, as her friend made exaggerated facial expressions.

William turned his attention towards Boy who immediately stopped his strange behaviour

"Em...it's nothing," he said, looking down at the table.

"It is," Violet interrupted, "otherwise why would you be making those faces?"

"Thanks Violet!" Boy snapped, annoyed at his friend's lack of subtlety.

"Come on Boy, spit it out," William said.

"Well..." Boy began, "I'm not sure about going to the estate just yet. I...I don't think it's a good idea."

William shifted in his seat.

"And why not?" he asked.

"It's just well… I know the Watchers aren't the brightest but they aren't stupid either, I've spent twelve years finding that out. They know that we know where Macula and Violet's Dad are. They know we know about the eyes and the Archers' experiments too so they'll be on high alert to anyone going in or out of the estate. I really don't think it is a good idea to go there first. I know you want Macula and Violet wants her Dad back but they'll be expecting that and we'll have walked straight into a trap."

"I kinda agree with Boy," Violet said, quietly just as William Archer stood up and began pacing the room.

"Boy, I'm impressed," he said, after a few minutes, "I was going to run into this like a bull in a china shop. All thought of Macula has clearly clouded my vision. I see now I've been selfish. This can't be just about me, or what I want. It has to be about Perfect. Perhaps we need some lateral thinking."

"I think we need a diversion," Boy said, "Maybe that way we can free Perfect and Macula and Violet's Dad all at the same time."

"What do you have in mind?" William replied, taking to his seat once more.

Violet and William listened intently as Boy outlined his plan and by that evening they had formulated the first part of 'Project Perfect'. William Archer took to his den to find all the research he had on reversing his brothers' blinding concoction.

"I knew I had these notes somewhere," he said, carrying a bunch of papers back up from his basement. "I'd been working on reversing the effects of their tablets for a while, but abandoned it thinking it was a task too big for one man. Perhaps it's not too big for one man, one boy and one girl though. However, I'm not altogether sure this mixture will work on the tea. They didn't have that in my day."

"I'm sure they use the same stuff in the tea as they did in the tablets. They just probably use more of it," Violet smiled.

"Good point Violet," William replied, as he cleared a space on his desk and began to pull out glass flasks from all sorts of nooks and crannies.

Violet and Boy tried to pick up on some sleep needed if they were to be successful in the next part of their plan as William Archer the scientist sprung to life. He argued with himself as he worked about the amounts of this or that needed to reverse the effects of the tea. Later that night he gently shook the pair from their dreams and handed over a flask of greenish pink liquid.

"I do hope this works," he smiled, wiping the sweat from his brow.

"Brilliant," Boy said, sleepily taking hold of the flask, "we'll be back fingers crossed by tomorrow evening."

"What if we can't find the factory?" Violet asked.

"We'll find it," Boy replied.

"I'll have the old crew rounded up for your return," William said, "it should take a day or two for the mixture to work so we have time to get the Reimaginator back into action."

William gave them both a big hug as they left his house under the cover of darkness.

"Sometimes I really don't like adults," Violet whispered as they edged along the dark street, "but sometimes I love them. I don't know why but their hugs always make me feel safe."

"I wouldn't know, that was my first one," Boy replied, checking round the corner ahead.

His first hug! Violet couldn't believe it. She followed

behind her friend in a somber silence the whole way to the Archer Brothers shop.

CHAPTER 26

Merrill Marx Tea Makers

"I thought we were meant to be looking for the factory. What are we doing here?" Violet asked, as Boy pulled her into the bushes directly opposite the Archer's shop.

"We are but for now we're waiting," he replied.

"For what?"

"You'll see," he smiled, and continued his surveillance.

Violet sat back in the bushes, found a comfortable spot and refused to talk to Boy; his response was vague, why couldn't he just tell her the plan? It was a dark night but the air was warm, and the lonely hoot of an owl resting somewhere above occupied her mind. Hours passed and she'd just nodded off when Boy yanked her sleeve dragging her from her slumber.

"This is it," he whispered, "we have to go now. Follow me."

Violet, half asleep, followed her friend from the safety of the bushes out into the dark street. There was a faint outline of a van parked outside the Archer's shop. A Watcher sat idly on the bonnet, the back doors of the vehicle hung open.

Boy got onto his knees and crawled across the tarmac towards the van. Pebbles and stones dug into her flesh as Violet followed suit. Reaching the back door of the van, Boy signalled to climb aboard. He wanted her to get into the Watchers van, was he mad? She shook her head and turned to crawl back. Boy grabbed her ankle. His grip was firm and his eyes wild and strong. He pointed again. She climbed aboard.

It was dark and she almost collided with a large wooden barrel on her left. She put her hands out. There was another barrel on her right and a narrow space between them. She squeezed in through the middle and hid behind the right hand barrel. Boy followed her lead and slipped in behind the left one. It was pitch black inside and her heart beat rapidly. Boy was invisible in the darkness. She shoved out her foot until she touched his. Her heartbeat steadied. She rested her head against the cold sides of the van and waited.

It seemed as if they had been there ages when a door banged. Violet jumped. Boy's hand quickly grabbed her ankle and squeezed. Footsteps crunched across the gravel and without a word the back door of the van slammed shut. The pair were alone in the dark. The van rocked as a Watcher climbed into the driver's seat and it rocked again as another got in on the passenger side.

"That pair are in foul form these days!" the driver snarled, as the engine sprung to life.

"I've never seen them any other way," the passenger said, as he rolled down the window, with one enormous snort he sucked all the snot from his nose and sent it flying into the air.

Cobbled streets caused the barrels to dance round the back almost crushing Violet on numerous occasions. They'd been travelling for a long time when the driver suddenly slammed on the brakes. The large barrels raced forward banging Violet roughly on the elbow. The pain seared she bit her tongue to stop the scream. The Watchers climbed out of the front. Boy poked his head through the seats and looked around.

"You okay?" he whispered, pulling back inside.

She nodded.

"We're here. We have to get out now."

Silently he slipped through the seats, into the front and out the driver's door. Alone in the van panic took over pain. Boy signalled frantically at her through the front window. She let go of her elbow and climbed swiftly through the gap in the seats. Once outside Boy grabbed her hand and raced for cover round the corner of a large stone shed. They were in the middle of the countryside and it was impossible to know whether it was Perfect or No Mans Land or somewhere else altogether. Dusk was breaking over the surrounding hills and the morning light brought new unease.

"How do you know this is the place?" Violet whispered.

"Take a look," Boy said, pointing back around the side of the shed.

Violet did as instructed. Another stone building greeted her. It was larger than the one they hid behind and had definitely seen better days. The walls were crumbling and the building was pockmarked with holes where bricks had fallen out or disintegrated. The windows that weren't broken were covered in a film of misty condensation blocking any view of the inside. Steam bellowed from every nook and cranny, making the place look like a rocket ready to launch. A sign made in colourful letters rested over the rickety wooden door. It once read *Merrill Marx Toy Makers* but the "oy" was roughly crossed out in black brush strokes and replaced with a scribbled "ea".

"Merrill Marx Tea Makers?" Violet whispered, "Who's Merrill Marx?"

"Not a tea maker!" Boy replied angrily, "Merrill Marx is living in No Mans Land. I remember when I was young the nurses would sometimes take us on a trip to his toyshop. They never bought us anything but I loved looking at all the toys. He'd all sorts. Toys you couldn't even imagine."

"So the Archers robbed his factory from him?"

"Don't worry Violet," Boy smiled, "we'll rob it back."

Violet followed Boy round the smaller shed and they slipped inside through an open doorway at the back. The place was full to the brim of barrels, just like the ones in the Watchers van. The words *Merrill Marx Tea Makers* were scrawled in rough handwriting across the front of them all.

"I've seen the Watchers delivering these," Boy whispered, lifting the lid from one to peer inside, "They always do it late at night. They leave a few barrels at the Archer's and then drop a few more round Perfect."

"They must be for carrying the tea," Violet said.

Boy was about to reply when voices approached from outside. Both ran for cover behind a stack of barrels just as two burly Watchers entered the shed.

"So I told old Eddie that if he wanted me working for him no more he better show a bit of respect or he'd have it," one of the Watchers laughed.

"And wha happened?"

"Well he cried like a snifflin' dog, he did. Begged me to stay and all!"

"So why you still workin' the barrels with me den?"

"Cause I likes the barrels," the Watcher snapped, as he picked one up and began to roll it out of the shed.

"Ya showed old Eddie alright!" the other one laughed, grabbing another barrel and heading outside.

Boy slipped out from hiding and ran to a window.

"They're rolling them into the factory Violet," he whispered, "I think I've got an idea."

Violet shook her head as Boy explained what he had in mind.

"It's the only way Violet. The factory is over flowing with Watchers. There's no other way in."

"But they'll feel our weight Boy. They'll know there is something inside."

"No they won't Violet they're rolling them. We'll brace

ourselves against the sides to make sure we don't move and anyway both those Watchers seem a little slow. We'll be fine!" Boy smiled, climbing inside the closest barrel to the door.

"I'm not sure Boy," Violet protested climbing inside the one beside his, "this seems a little…"

"Ssh Violet, they're coming back. You'll be fine. Remember when you saved me, you're way braver than I am," Boy said, looking across the yard, "Now quick pass me your lid!"

Violet handed it over and ducked down into the base of her barrel.

"You'll be fine," he whispered, as the space plunged into darkness, "Just brace yourself and wait for me to come get you."

There was a gently thud as Boy closed his own lid then silence. Violet's heart pounded in her chest. Footsteps approached from across the yard, soft at first they got louder until the Watchers were standing right by the barrels. There was a loud bang. Violet stopped breathing.

"Those blasted lids. Have to give 'em a right wallop to stay on," a voice said, from directly above.

They were only an arms reach from danger. Suddenly she was jerked forward until she was lying on her side, her knees touching her chin.

> "This one's a bit heavy, wonder if them Perfectionists is drinkin' all the tea?"

> "Don't say that when de bosses around. That'd get them right angry and they're cross enough lately."

> "Right foul buggers they are," Violet's Watcher spat as she began to roll across the yard.

Her head spun round and round like she was in a washing machine. Imagine how clothes feel? From this moment on she would only wear dirty clothes. Her stomach churned. The narrow space of the barrel grew narrower. It was extremely hot. Sweat rolled off her forehead, drips slipped down her back and even her arms oozed salty drops. She would not get sick.

The outside world disappeared and she was plunged into a solitary torture. She was faint. She couldn't lose control so close to danger. She'd let Boy, William and her family down. Suddenly, as her head spun in despair, the barrel stopped and she was jerked upright. Her feet were back to where they should be, below her head.

She didn't move a muscle. The Watchers chatted for a few

moments above her then moved off, their voices fading into the distance. Violet waited but Boy didn't appear. He'd said to hold on for him but what if something had happened? Just as she was about to move the lid popped off above her.

"Come on," Boy whispered, looking into the barrel, "they've gone."

His face was green and covered in tell tale droplets. There was also a slight sickly smell.

"Are you okay?" Violet asked, climbing from her barrel.

"Fine."

"It's just..."

"I'm fine Violet!"

"You've been sick," she smiled, suddenly feeling much better.

"No I haven't. Now come on this is no time for games," Boy snapped, popping back on the lid.

Violet tried not to laugh as she followed her friend across the room full of barrels. Rows of white coats and hats hung off hooks on the wall opposite. Putting on one of each, Boy handed another set to Violet.

"They all wear them," he explained, "we'll blend in."

Suddenly a loud horn rang through the factory and the barrels around them began to rattle. Violet grabbed Boy's coat sleeve and pointed. The barrels were sitting on a conveyor belt, like the ones in airports and had started to move. There was a hole in the wall on the opposite side of the room and they were being shunted in uniform towards it. The factory was now full of noise. Beeps, whooshes and swooshes flew around them and Violet couldn't hear a word Boy was saying. Frustrated he pulled her towards a door at the side of the room and pointed.

"WE HAVE TO GO OUT THERE!" he roared just as the noises stopped.

Boy's voice boomed from the room. Violet froze. They both stood terrified waiting for the Watchers to arrive.

CHAPTER 27

William's Potion

Violet shivered, 'It's someone walking on your grave' her Dad always said. She shook off the thought. Death was too close to joke about standing on the floor of the Watchers factory. Boy looked uneasy too though it could have been from his barrel rolling adventure. Violet eyed the door, then Boy, then the door again. Neither moved and after a few minutes she signed relief.

"I don't think they heard you," she whispered.

Boy breathed for the first time in a few moments washing away some of the odd blue colour that rested on his face. He was about to speak when the horn went off once more and the barrels began to move.

"I think it must be on a cycle," he whispered as the noise stopped, "It's every five minutes I'd say. Next time it goes we'll open the door and get out of here; nobody will hear us in that racket. We need to find where they make the tea."

"Will we split up?" Violet asked, "It might be quicker."

"Okay I'll go right, you go left."

Violet nodded and they both waited nervously for the horn to sound again. On cue Boy opened the door. Suddenly the room flooded with steam. It was blinding and Violet's eyes stung in the prickly hot air. Boy had already disappeared into the fog on her right, so she made her way gingerly from the barrel room onto the steaming factory floor. A haze of shadowy Watchers passed by busy with their duties. Reassuringly they also wore white coats and hats, Violet pulled her cap further down to blend in with the crowd.

The Watchers sped through the space well used to the foggy atmosphere. One of them brushed lightly past Violet while looking down at a chart. Her stomach churned. His face was wrinkly, so wrinkly it was hard to see his features lost to rolls of puffy pink skin. He looked like the tips of Violet's fingers after she'd spent too long in the bath.

The noise stopped again. She had to concentrate. She had a task to do. There was a line of barrels just up ahead. If she followed them they might lead her to the tea. She reached the carousel just as a group of Watchers approached. Quickly she turned her back and pretended to inspect the line.

"Everything alright?" a Watcher said, stopping just short of her.

"Oh em...yes," Violet replied, in the deepest voice possible, "just em... checking the barrels. Looks good!"

The Watcher nodded and walked away. Her knees shook as she waited for him to disappear into the fog then hurried onwards. Her lungs burned, it was hard to breath let alone see in the thick steam.

Keeping close to the carousel she was suddenly in the middle of the factory floor. It was a large circular area alive with activity. The horn went off again. This time the first five barrels in line moved forward into the circular space and were each shunted down a different shoot of the carousel to separate workstations. Each barrel was surrounded by three enormous steaming kettles linked by metal pipes to a huge tank suspended above the factory floor. It had to be the tea. Once the barrels were at their stations, the kettles tipped over one by one filling each with steaming hot liquid. Once full, the noise stopped, a Watcher secured the lid and the five barrels were shunted back out onto the main carousel. They moved off in a different direction and the next five waited their turn.

Violet had found the tea, now she just needed to find Boy. Suddenly someone grabbed her from behind and a hand flew up over her mouth.

"Ssh," Boy whispered, "Follow me and don't ask any questions."

Violet nodded and calmly followed her friend towards a door straight in front of them. Walking confidently Boy looked like he belonged, why couldn't she be that brave? He opened the door and Violet stepped inside. The room was dark. It took a moment for her eyes to adjust. Suddenly she screamed but Boy's hand was in place to muffle the sound.

"They're just dolls," he whispered, "I found this place when I left you. I think it's where they test the tea but it must have been the doll room when this place was a toy factory."

The room was lined in shelving, packed with baby body parts. Rows of tiny, hairless, heads stared unblinking from plastic boxes. Mini arms hung off hooks and fatty dismembered legs dangled from drawers. Reams of paper and flasks of moldy tea rested on the workbenches.

"Did you see the tank?" Boy asked.

Violet nodded.

"It's the tea. There's a stairs that goes up to it," he said, "but it's full of Watchers and I'm not sure both of us would pass unnoticed…"

"Well then it's up to one of us," Violet interrupted.

"It's not that easy Violet," Boy replied. "There are Watchers everywhere. I don't want them to know that we've been here, otherwise our whole plan will be ruined. We can't be seen. We need to cause a diversion, I just don't know how."

"What about the barrels?" Violet said excitedly, "Maybe if we cause a blockage in the barrel room the whole operation will stop working. It's all connected. The kettles will pour into nothing, there'll be steaming tea all over the floor. The Watchers will be running about the place in a panic."

Boy took a minute.

"That's brilliant Violet, it just might work," he eventually smiled, "I think you've been hanging around No Mans Land too long. They won't want you back in Perfect now!"

"Hopefully there won't be a Perfect when we're finished."

For the next hour the pair planned their attack. It had to be perfect. It was decided Boy would go to the barrel room and cause the diversion. Being a boy, he argued, meant he was stronger and better able to lift the barrels. His logic didn't make sense since the barrels were empty and he was skinny. Boys were sometimes stupid. Once the diversion was working it was her job to climb the stairs undetected and drop the flask of William Archer's liquid into the tank of tea. Easy.

"Remember to wait for my signal," Boy said, as he left the room on the sounding of the horn.

Violet paced the floor. She'd always hated dolls even when she was younger. There was something scary about them. The plastic eyes followed her through the room. Imagine if they climbed out of their boxes and crawled after her? She shook off the image. She had to concentrate. A second horn had gone off since Boy left and still nothing happened. There was no signal. A third horn and nothing. Her heart pounded as she played with William Archer's flask. Just then a sharp screech bounced off the walls. It cut right through her. The signal! She ran to the door and opened it just in time to see the chaos.

Quickly she closed it again and rested her head against the cold metal. Placing the flask inside the waistband of her trousers, she took a deep breath and slipped out the room of dolls.

Watchers sprinted through the steam towards the carousel. Whatever Boy had done it worked. Kettles were pouring into empty space. Watchers rushed forward with buckets to catch the steaming liquid before it hit the floor. She looked out of place moving slowly through the madness so she sped up. The stairs was just ahead. She ran for it holding tightly to the flask through her coat. She'd just reached the first step when a hand grabbed her jacket.

"You! Come with me and take this," a wrinkly Watcher said, as he thrust a bucket into her hand.

The flask slipped. The conical glass moved rapidly down the leg of her trousers about to hit the floor. She dropped the bucket to grab it.

"What's wrong you stupid fool? Pick up that bucket and follow me. We're losing gallons of that blasted tea and you're playing with your pants!" the Watcher shouted.

Securing the flask once more in her waistband, Violet pulled down her cap and nodded. At the station she copied those around her and began to fill the bucket with tea. It smelt good, like ice cream and chocolate. Memories of all the glorious cups she shared in Perfect made her weak.

The tea was hypnotic. The tang of fizzy cola bottles hit her tongue and the tantalizing twist of ice cream and orange danced on her taste buds. She was swept away in a world of sweet sugar.

"Hurry up!" a Watcher growled, as Violet stopped to sniff the bucket, "You'd swear you never smelt that stuff before. What you say your name was again?"

Panic ripped away her sugary dreams. Her mind went blank as the Watcher stared. Ignoring his question, she filled the bucket and walked steadily back towards the barrel.

"Oi you sonny, I asked you a question!" the Watcher growled.

She kept walking her legs like wobbly jelly.

"Oi!" he shouted again, this time he was angry.

"Hey Bill shut your trap and get back to work. It's not the time for fightin!" another Watcher yelled.

"I ain't fightin mate!" Violet's attacker replied.

"It looks like fightin to me ya big over grown lump of lard!"

A roar rose up behind Violet. She turned. Her Watcher was running head long for a man at the opposite station. Seizing the opportunity, she dropped her bucket and raced for the stairs.

The Watchers now circled the fight. Violet sped unnoticed up the steps. Reaching the top she pulled the flask from her trousers. The landing was round and hugged the circumference of the tank. Violet ran around it but there was no opening to spill out the flask. A ladder on the side of the tank went up over the top of the steel cylinder. The Watchers were still focused on the fight but if any of them looked up they'd see her scaling the tank. She couldn't worry about that. She took the flask in her teeth and grabbed the metal steps. Quickly she climbed to the top of the giant container. The ground was miles below, her arms shook, dizziness hit her. She steadied for a minute.

There was a small circular handle like the steering wheel on top of the tank. She crawled towards it. Grabbing the handle she twisted. It was stiff at first but quickly loosened in her grip. Her heart pounded as the sounds of the fight reached up from the factory floor. She pulled back the handle with all her strength and it opened up into the tank. Ripping the cork from the flask, she kissed the murky glass and emptied the contents into the tea below. Then she closed up the door and climbed back down the ladder.

She descended the stairs avoiding the fight and made her way back towards the barrel room. Boy, as he said he would be, was waiting there. With a quick nod, she followed her friend through the steam towards the exit.

Once outside, the pair sprinted across the yard, hid their coats in a barrel in the smaller shed and ran as fast as they could away from the factory.

CHAPTER 28

A Powerful Fear

They didn't stop running until they were just outside the centre of No Mans Land.

"Did you...did you...?" Boy said, bending over by a tree to catch his breath.

"Yes," Violet panted.

"No one saw?"

"No I don't think so. They were all too busy with the fight."

Boy looked confused and Violet filled him in on her adventures on their way to William Archer's. It was early morning in No Mans Land and strangely all was quiet. There were hardly any stalls, nobody was begging and even the orphans had all but disappeared.

"That's her!" a woman snarled, rushing out from her lopsided home.

Another woman, about Violet's Mams age, grabbed her by the coat pulling Violet roughly back.

"The cheek of you!" the woman roared, "Don't you think we have it hard enough without setting the Watchers on us?"

"Let go of me," Violet screamed, "I haven't done anything!"

"Not yet young one but you're trying, you and that boyfriend of yours. Just leave us alone! We're as happy as can be expected here. We don't need any trouble!"

"She hasn't done anything," Boy shouted pulling Violet away from the woman.

"They're talking revolution in Will Archer's place all night and day. Know anything about that do you?" the woman said, almost nose to nose with Boy, her rancid breath licked his skin.

Quickly Boy grabbed Violet's arm and the pair ran off in the direction of William Archer's. They raced through the tiny streets and without knocking pushed open the door of the ramshakled house.

The room was full with people and they had to slip through

a sea of legs to get near the front of the gathering. Many were faces from the streets of No Mans Land but there were others Violet didn't know at all. Some were happy but most grunted and growled as William spoke at the top of the room. The place was stuffy and smelt of old men, Violet held her nose as she squeezed past another bulging belly.

"What about the Watchers?" a man shouted, from the back of the room.

"I'm not sure what will happen with them if I'm honest," William Archer said from his pulpit, an old wooden stool, "I think we may have to fight. I'm not a young man but I am willing to give my fists an airing if you are gents...oh and ladies of course."

"We'll never beat them," another man called.

"We will with a bit of luck," William replied, "I am banking on the fact that our friends and families in Perfect will join us once they see we're alive."

"And how do you propose they'll see us, hasn't that been the problem all along William? I think it's time to stop this talk. It's doing none of us any good. We're here to stay and it's about time some of us accepted that!"

"A man of your imagination stands defeated Fredrick?" William replied, looking straight into the eyes of the man who spoke, "they will see again, I promise you."

"Promises you can't keep old man!"

"He can keep them," Violet said, angrily stepping out from the crowd.

"Violet!" William exclaimed, jumping down from his chair, "Thank heavens you're alright. And Boy is he with you?"

"He's there," Violet said, pointing to her friend who had shyly stepped back into the crowd.

"How did you get on?" William whispered anxious.

Violet pulled the empty flask from her pants and handed it to the old man. Grabbing it in both hands, William held the bottle tightly to his chest, and inhaled long and deep.

"They'll see again," he shouted.

Jumping back onto the stool he shoved the flask into the air for all to see.

"My two little friends made sure of that!"

The room began to whisper. William stared out at the gathered crowd until all had fallen silent then he explained the tea factory plan.

"It'll take a few days, possibly two before the antidote begins to take effect. Then I assure you when we walk down the streets of Perfect our families will see us! After that we zap them with the Reimaginator and Perfect will fall."

"The what?" a voice laughed, at the end of the room.

"The Reimaginator," William repeated, "You see they are stealing our loved one's imaginations; that's how my brothers control them. Not only do they not see us because of that blasted tea but they also don't question anything. Our disappearance, the regime in Perfect; nothing seems out of the ordinary to them as they have lost the ability to question. They've lost independent thought."

"Well I'm delighted I stayed to hear you answer our questions William because now I know for sure that you are crazy. I'm out," a big burly man said, walking to the door.

Others began to move towards the exit passing out in silence.

"Why now William?" another man asked, "I mean I was

with you at the beginning but we all gave up. What's happened to bring back your fight?"

"It's Macula, Merrill. They have her. I gave up because I had nothing to fight for. I thought she'd left me. I didn't exist. Then with the help of Violet and Boy here I found out she's still alive. It's brought back the fight."

"Look we are in No Mans Land because we are different!" William shouted, addressing those slipping from the room, "Where has your imagination gone? Where is the fight? This is not Perfect but you are all acting like it is!"

"Grow up Archer! No Mans Land is our lot, what's the point in fighting? If you draw the Watchers down on us you'll have me to answer to!" a man roared at William as he left the house.

The crowd steadily filtered from the room and William Archer, accepting defeat, stepped down from the stool, crushed.

"They sound just like I did not so long ago," he said, his head in his hands, "they've lost the fight. If only my brothers knew they didn't need to steal imaginations to control us!"

Violet stepped forward.

"It's okay," she said, "we can still do it. I know it will be harder just us but we can do it."

"Violet," William smiled, looking up at her, "you're a lovely child. Your enthusiasm knows no bounds but in this case, three against many will not suffice."

"What about four?" someone said, stepping out from the shadows.

"Merrill! I presumed you'd left with the others?"

"No William, I thought about it I must confess," Merrill smiled, "but I missed the old William and the adventures we had taking on your brothers. My toys serve me well but they are not a substitute for my family. It's time to get them back! Where do I sign up?"

William Archer stood up from his stool and wrapped his arms around his old friend.

"Merrill Marx?" Violet asked.

"Why yes, have we met before?"

"No but I have just come from your factory."

Violet was filling Merrill in on their adventures, when Boy, who had been sitting quietly by the window, rose and walked towards the group.

"I know where we can get an army," he said.

All attention turned towards him.

"They might be a little small but they'll have lots of energy," he smiled.

CHAPTER 29

Little Helpers

After a quick nap, Violet and Boy spent the rest of the day discussing their plans, while William and Merrill worked on the Reimaginator. By nightfall the machine hummed.

"I knew it'd only take a tweak," William smiled, proudly polishing the brass, "now all we need are a few imaginations and she'll be purring again."

"We're going to sort that out now," Boy smiled, "they should be in bed by eight."

"Are you sure this plan will work?" Merrill asked.

"Of course Mr. Marx," Violet replied, "Nothings ever difficult for children, adults are much more complicated..."

"You remember the meeting point William?" Boy interrupted, "We should reach it by morning."

"Don't worry Boy, we'll be there with this old girl."

Boy and Violet said goodbye to their friends and, for the second time in as many days, left William Archer's house under the cover of darkness. Violet followed Boy predicting every turn they took; No Mans Land was no longer a mystery. The streets now were quiet, the Watchers patrolling more vigorously than ever before. The pair snuck round corners until they eventually stood by the huge iron gates. They squeezed through the partial opening and around to the side door. After a quick jig of the handle, they were standing in the enormous hallway of the orphanage.

"This way," Boy whispered, tiptoeing down the tiled floor.

The place was dark and cold. Fear crawled up Violet's spine. They reached a wooden stairwell and climbed two floors, then walked down another hallway to a set of wooden double doors.

"Be really quiet," Boy mouthed, pushing them open.

He slipped in through the narrow gap, Violet in toe.

"Stay here," he ordered.

Doing as told, Violet stood by the base of a metal-framed bunk bed. A small thin figure moved beneath a threadbare blanket in the bottom bed. There were at least twenty bunks in the oversized room, all occupied with similar small figures.

The air was cold and wisps of foggy breath danced in front of her nose. Moans and groans followed Boy as he quietly made his way from bed to bed pulling each child gently from their sleep. When he finally got back to Violet, the room hummed with whispers.

"Shush," Boy said, putting a finger to his lips, "I'm going to turn on the light now. I have a favour to ask. Please don't make a sound or the nurses will come rushing down here and we know what will happen then."

The room filled with shushes and giggles.

"Not a sound," Boy warned, switching on the light.

There was a faint flicker from above. Then another, this one lasting a little longer, then the light came to life. Forty miniature, messy haired heads peered out from under dirty sheets.

"What is it Boy?" a little girl in one of the upper bunks asked, grabbing the railing that ran round the edge of her bed, "is it Santy?"

"No Monica," Boy smiled, "It's not Santa. I have a job that I want you to help me with. If it works you'll go back to your families."

"Just me?" Monica asked.

227

"No I need everybody's help," Boy smiled.

"Really, we'll really go home?" a fella a little younger than Boy said, jumping up on his mattress, "Like home, home Boy? You're not joking are ya?"

"No, no, I'm not joking. You'll go home, I promise."

"Well then I'm in, I don't care what it is!"

"You can come live in my house Boy," Monica said, "cause you don't have one."

"Thanks Mon," Boy smiled, lifting the little girl into his arms, "Now listen. I want you all to think about this really hard 'cause it's going to be dangerous."

"Wohoo, danger!" another little boy laughed, jumping up and down on his bed.

Boy and Violet spent the next few hours explaining the plan to the orphans. Each was as excited as the next and it took a lot of "shushing" to avoid waking the nurses. By ten that night everyone was dressed, ready and waiting.

"I really hope this works Boy," Violet whispered.

"It will."

"You know," she continued, as she helped stuff decoy

pillows under the empty blankets, "you can come live in my house too."

"Thanks Violet," he smiled.

A few minutes later, room ready and lights off, the army of forty strong slipped out into the hallway. Surprisingly the children remained deadly quiet and they left the orphanage without a hitch.

"I thought we'd never get them out that quietly," Violet whispered, as Boy closed the entrance doors.

"They know what the nurses are like. If we got caught we'd all be in for a beating!" Boy smiled.

In the yard they split into five groups. Violet, Boy and three of the older kids were in charge of one each. Boy's group would lead the way with Violet's taking up the rear.

"If we get divided," Boy whispered, just before he left, "we'll meet at the entrance to the Ghost Estate. You all know how to get there?"

Everyone nodded.

One by one the groups left until it was Violet's turn. The coast was clear. She beckoned the others forward. The night was dark, pitch black and it was hard to spot Watchers as they navigated the lonely streets. Violet stuck to the walls travelling as much in the shadows as possible. The others were nowhere to be seen.

"We need to go faster," she whispered.

They picked up the pace and were now jogging through the alleyways. The group coped well and were making good ground. Everything was running smoothly until a loud smack filled the street followed quickly by a high-pitched cry.

"She pushed me," a little girl roared, holding her elbow, "she pushed me. My elbowwwww!"

"Shush," Violet whispered, rushing back to the girl's side, "Shusssh. You have to be quiet. The Watchers will catch us."

"But my elbow is sore," the girl cried, tears streaming down her face.

"Please stop crying."

"Oi who goes there?" a deep voice shouted.

There was a figure at the other end of the street, barely visible in the darkness. Violet turned quickly to the girl accused of pushing and grabbed the shawl that wrapped her shoulders. Throwing the tattered material over her own head she whispered to the others to hide and grabbed the hand of the sobbing girl.

"You have to be brave and you have to agree with everything I say. Understand?"

The girl shook her head and even more tears streamed down her face.

"What are you two doing out here?" the Watcher snarled, moving down the road towards them.

"My sister fell," Violet replied, her voice shaky.

"I can see that but it doesn't answer my question little girl."

"We were at the market," Violet stuttered, pulling the shawl tighter around her, "we're on our way home."

"The market closed a few hours ago, it's taken you a long time to get back?"

"We got lost."

"Where do you live?" the Watcher asked, moving closer.

Violet's heart stopped. What were the street names in No Mans Land? Her cheeks burned. Her mind was blank. What were the street names?

"Moore Street," the little girl sobbed.

Her breath caught, she squeezed the girl's hand. The Watcher looked at Violet then at the little girl without uttering a word.

"Well you better be getting back there then," he said eventually, "haven't you heard there's a curfew in No Mans Land?"

"Yes, I'm sorry Sir," Violet replied, looking at her feet, "we'll go now. It won't happen again. I promise."

They slipped past the giant. Violet's heart pounded so hard the Watcher must have heard.

"Oi?" he called after them, as they neared the street corner.

Violet stiffened. Running away would make things worse. She turned slowly on the spot.

"You sure you know where you're going this time?"

"Yes," she answered, almost whispering.

"Moore Street is that way," he said, pointing to his left.

"Oh em...thanks," Violet replied, and quickly took the direction he'd indicated.

The Watcher stood on the spot, his eyes suspiciously followed them until they rounded the corner. The pair kept walking incase he pursued. After a few minutes, when they were in the clear, Violet loosened her grip on the girl and stopped. Lowering onto her honkers she let out a long slow breath.

"I'm sorry Violet," the little girl said, putting an arm around her, "I didn't mean to make you sad."

"You didn't," Violet whispered, "You saved us."

The pair waited for a while in the shadow of a doorway before returning to the group.

"You all did great," Violet smiled, sounding as positive as possible, "Now let's go, the others will be wondering where we got to."

CHAPTER 30

Return To The Room Of Imaginations

They resumed their journey this time without a sound. They reached the entrance to the Ghost Estate shaken and late. The other groups sat huddled by the wall barely visible. Violet jumped as Boy ran out from the darkness.

"Boy," she wheezed, "please don't do that. I thought you were another Watcher."

"What do you mean another?"

"We met one on the street. I don't think he noticed anything though. I said we were lost and he seemed to believe me."

"Well we better not wait any longer, just in case he was suspicious."

Boy ran back to ready the others and one by the one the groups slipped off into the Ghost Estate. Violet and her gang were again left 'til last.

"You have to be really brave in here," she whispered to the orphans, "you're going to feel very sad but you have to promise me you won't cry."

"Why will we be sad?" a boy of about seven asked.

"I don't know but it's not a real feeling. It's just something that happens in there," Violet said, pointing through the gates, "Once you leave the feeling will go."

"What if it doesn't?"

"It will," Violet said, looking at the dark entrance, "I promise."

When all the orphans swore they'd be brave, Violet turned to face the estate.

"Okay," she whispered, "let's go."

They passed in through the cement pillars and immediately the weight of the world collapsed on Violet's shoulders. Everything bad that had happened jumped to the front of her mind. Her mother and father, Boy with no parents, Macula Archer locked in her room. Her pace slowed, her shoulders slumped, tears readied round her eyes. There was a short tug on her sleeve. The little girl from before stared up at her. Her eyes huge against her pale skin.

"You said it's not real Violet is it?"

Violet looked back at the group, all were crying. Her heart surged. She had to be strong, for them.

"No it's not real," she soothed, and squeezed the girl's hand.

A thick fog hung low over the ground swallowing the other groups one by one. Violet shivered. The estate was eerily quiet as they tiptoed through. Just as Boy predicted; almost all the Watchers were busy surveying the streets of Perfect. With extra patrols now watching No Mans Land, the Ghost Estate was relatively clear. Urging her orphans forward they increased their pace. They stuck to the road a safe distance from the sleeping eye plants that still haunted Violet's dreams.

A lonely lamppost yellowed the haze ahead and she shepherded the group towards it. The place turned icy cold. Her skin crawled like a million maggots fought to break out her insides. A shadow moved through the mist. Violet stopped halting the group. A figure stood alone under the light. She whispered to the orphans to stay put and ventured across the sparse grass.

"Who's there?"

"It's me Boy," Violet whispered.

"About time," he snapped, "everyone's already in the tunnel. There's Watchers about. Let's go!"

Violet signalled her group forward and they followed Boy across the grass, through the turnstile into the graveyard. Immediately the sadness lifted leaving fear in its wake. An overgrown path led them through the centre of the cemetery. The smell of rot soaked the air forcing everyone to grab their nostrils. Tombstones hovered in the mist on either side and an eerie presence hung over Violet's shoulder as if the dead were watching. One of the younger girls began to cry and the pace increased unconsciously. The gates were just ahead. Their walk turned to a jog and as one little girl let out a shrill cry, all five sprinted for the exit.

"Ssh, you have to be quiet," Boy snapped, standing just outside the gates, "follow me quickly, everyone's waiting inside."

The orphans looked at Violet as Boy disappeared into the tunnel.

"In there?" one of them shivered.

"We'll be fine," Violet soothed, leading them forwards.

The tunnel was black and it took a moment before outlines appeared huddled by the wall. All the orphans were back together and the safety of numbers appeared to calm the nerves. After a quick break they moved off under Boy's instruction, in the direction of the Watcher's den. The air was thick with damp making it a struggle to breathe.

"I'm frightened," a small boy said, grabbing Violet's hand.

She smiled and squeezed his palm; it normally worked when her Mam did it. She missed having her Mam and Dad take care of her. Now she was the adult, she had to take care of this boy and all the other boys and girls in the tunnel. She wasn't ready. She didn't want to grow up.

"Everybody back against the wall," Boy whispered urgently.

Her unconscious took over and she forced the group back, quickly she raced up the line quietening the crowd. Her heart pounded but she could do this. She could be just as strong as Boy. He needed her to be now more than ever. As the groups stood statue still, Boy peered around a corner up ahead.

"They've gone," he whispered, rejoining the others.

They picked up the pace and made steady progress towards the Archer's shop. On reaching the Watcher's empty den they stopped.

"We'll leave everybody here," Boy said, to two of the older boys, "you take care of them. You'll hear the Watchers if they're coming but I think we have a few hours left before they'll be back. Me and Violet are going to break into the Archer's storeroom. We'll come back for you then."

Violet stared at Boy. Were they not going to break into the Archers together? What happened to safety in numbers?

"You'll be fine," Boy said, reading her thoughts.

"I know I will," Violet replied quickly, "It's you I'm worried about."

Violet swallowed deeply then followed her friend out onto the dark stairwell that led to the Archer's storeroom. Boy stayed two steps ahead, his stride longer, and she struggled to keep up with his pace. What if the Archers were there - or worse the Watchers? She could cope with the Archers; they were ancient, but the Watchers were big and muscley. She'd never take them, even with Boys help. Quickly they reached the top of the stairs and Boy began pulling in vain on the brick handle. The door to the Archer's was locked.

"What now?" Violet asked, sure they would have to go back.

"We wait."

"For what?"

"For one of the Watchers to come back."

"But they'll catch us!"

"Not if we catch them first,"

Boy held up a strange object.

"The torch?" Violet said surprised.

"I hid it in the estate incase we ever needed it again," he smiled.

Violet would have smiled back but how on earth was the torch going to save them from the Watchers?

"What if there's more than one of them Boy?"

"There'll only be one. Fists is lazy, he normally sneaks off work long before the others. I reckon he'll be back here soon. We clobber him and get the keys."

"I hope you're right," Violet sighed. sliding down the wall onto the floor.

"Sure I'm never wrong!" Boy smiled.

It seemed like hours passed resting against the cold stone. Her head spun. She would have slept, her body almost weak with tiredness, had her mind let her. Suddenly keys jangled from behind the door. Nerve endings sparked, Violet climbed up from the floor ready to pounce.

"Blasted keys," a gruff voice snarled.

Boy moved swiftly across the space and stood, torch held high, just inside the entrance. The lock turned. Slowly the door swung open. Fists was bent over fiddling with the keys, he didn't see Boy swing for his head. There was a loud clatter, a howl of pain and he fell to the floor.

"Oi you mangy, wriggling, dirty, maggot!" a huge Watcher roared, as he rushed through the door grabbing Boy by the hair.

Violet froze to her spot by the wall. The Watcher didn't see her and Boy signalled her to hide as he struggled with the beast.

"I knew we'd catch you someday ya ugly orphan. No wonder your parents didn't want ya. I'm going to rip you to shreds."

Boy kicked his capture in the shin. He tried to run but the Watcher grabbed him, clattering him hard against the wall. Her friend's lifeless body was flung roughly over the Watcher's shoulder. As the giant oaf turned his back Violet picked up the torch and ran. Boy was in the way. If she swung she'd hit him.

The Watcher disappeared down the stairwell. The keys hung idle in the door above Fist's head. Grabbing them Violet slipped down the stairs. If the Watcher discovered the orphans they were goners.

Light trickled into the stairwell highlighting the figures ahead. Boy was still unconscious. Violet held her breath, close enough now that the Watcher might hear. He pounded into the room below. Where were the screams? She tiptoed in after him. The room was empty. The orphans were gone. The Watcher strode across the floor and flung Boy's body onto the cold stone. She winced as her friend's head smashed off the ground. Her mind on Boy, she didn't notice the Watcher turn. He stared straight at her. Veins running down the side of his bald head pulsed under pressure. Roaring, he made a surge for Violet his fist firm. She couldn't move. Arms, legs, wake up!

Suddenly hundreds of small bodies rushed out from cupboards, beds and boxes to grab hold of the Watcher's ankles. He kicked in fury but the orphans held tight. The scene was manic, still Violet's body wouldn't respond. Everyone was shouting at her. They were pointing and shouting. What was it? Her hand, they were pointing at her hand. The torch. She still had the torch. Snapping from her trance, noise filled the room.

"The torch, the torch, Violet the torch!"

She sprung to life. Tightening her grip she steadied the solid wood in her hands. The Watcher moved quickly, his pace slowed only a little by the orphans. She was screaming then running. Paces from him she lifted the torch. With all the force she could muster, she slammed the wooden stick down on top of the Watcher's bald head. There was a loud groan and the giant crashed solidly to the floor. On automatic, she kept running and tripped over his sprawling body. Then the orphans ambushed her. Like a soccer player who'd scored the winning goal, they screamed and jumped around her.

"You saved us, you saved us," they cried.

"Boy!" Violet roared, her friend's image suddenly springing to mind.

Ignoring the celebrations she rushed to his side. He was still unconscious.

"He's breathing, someone help me," she said, grabbing his ankles.

They lifted Boy onto one of the beds. Ensuring he was okay, Violet covered him in a blanket in case the Watchers came back. She turned to the group who were now a little calmer.

"We still have a job to do," she said, "Follow me!"

Quickly and as quietly as possible she ushered everyone up the steps. Fists was still unconscious as they tiptoed past into the Archer's storeroom.

"What are they?" a boy asked, pointing to the jars of colour.

"They're imaginations," Violet replied, loud enough for all to hear, "we have to take one each. Be careful when you're carrying them. We can't break any."

Everyone stood back afraid. Then one of the older boys stepped forward and walked the length of the corridor inspecting the lids of the jars. He stopped and pulled one from the shelf. Reading it carefully, he held the glass aloft.

"It's my dad's," he said to the group.

Amazed, the rest began to scour the shelves for their loved ones. Violet was helping a little girl when a jar caught her eye. Light pink and purple hues flooded the glass. *Rose Brown 02.02.11*, her mother's name written in tiny type. Shaking, she took the jar gently from the shelf. Boy should be with her now. She needed him. With him she was safe and everything would be alright. Without him? No she wouldn't think about that now.

She cradled the glass to her chest and helped the last of the orphans. Once everyone had an imagination, they dragged

Fists' unconscious body into the storeroom. Locking the door, they snuck back down the stairwell. Chimes of glass coloured the darkness.

"Be a bit quieter," a voice whispered, up from the room below.

Boy! It was his voice. He was sitting upright on the Watcher's bed as they entered the den.

"You're alive," Violet laughed, throwing herself around him.

"Violet, my head, it's still sore you know!"

"Oh I'm sorry. I was afraid..."

"A mangy Watcher's not going to kill me," he interrupted, wobbling to his feet.

He put his hands out to balance against the wall and Violet slipped in under his armpit.

"Lean on me," she whispered.

He smiled and steadied against her shoulder.

"We have them," she said, turning so Boy could see the orphans proudly holding their jars, "we're ready for William."

"We better hurry then," Boy replied groggily.

As quickly as possible they slipped through the winding tunnels and out into the Ghost Estate; their pace slowed a little by injury. Everyone held an imagination except Boy. As they crept past the house where her father was held Violet hugged the jar in her hands. Even if her parents were a little mad, she was lucky to have them.

"There's something up," Boy whispered. as they neared the estate entrance.

"What do you mean?" Violet asked.

He picked up a stone and fired it at one of the windows. The glass smashed, the sound reverberating through the estate.

"Boy! What are you doing? You'll get us caught."

Violet spun on the spot. There wasn't a stir from the houses, not a sound. Nothing happened. The eerie silence sent a shiver through her soul.

"There's nobody here," Boy said, "they've all gone. Everyone"

"Why?" Violet asked, keeping her voice as even as she could.

"I don't know, but we need to get back to William."

The group increased their pace. They passed through the Ghost Estate and out into No Mans Land, which was empty too. The Watchers who patrolled earlier had gone and not a soul walked the town. Curtains moved behind window frames as they slipped along the streets. They were being watched. They sped through the market square past empty stalls and towards the entrance to No Mans Land. The large, barbed wire pillars stood out just ahead. Two figures paced back and forth by their base.

William Archer and Merrill Marx turned in unison.

"Boy, Violet! We were so worried," William said, running to greet his friends.

"What's happened?" Boy asked.

"What is it?" Violet said catching her breath, "The Watchers- they've all gone!"

"They know there's something up," Merrill replied, "one of the No Mans Landers told them."

"But why would someone do that?" Violet asked angrily.

"They're afraid Violet," William replied, "fear does funny things to folk."

"But they're No Mans Landers. They're meant to be different..."

"Maybe not so different after all," William sighed.

"We have to do something! We have the imaginations. We're ready."

"I know Violet," William replied, "but we don't stand a chance now. There aren't enough of us."

"But if we stuck to the plan, if we could give the people back their imaginations there would be," Boy interrupted.

"We can't get near the people," Merrill sighed, "The Watchers have barricaded the main roads to Perfect. There's no way in."

Merrill walked away defeated. Violet looked at William then back at the jar in her hands. After all they'd done, everything was crashing down around them.

"This can't be it Boy," she pleaded.

For the first time since she'd met him, he looked lost. She slumped down by one of the pillars. Everything was gone. Her mother's imagination floated oblivious through the jar. She'd never see her Mam again. She'd probably start a new family, a perfect one. Violet would be wiped from her memory. Her Dad, she'd probably never see him either. She'd be just like Boy and William. She'd be alone. Suddenly in all the despair an idea hit her.

"Your mother, Iris, she lives on a side road just outside the town," she said, looking straight at William Archer.

"Leave her out of this Violet," William replied sharply.

"But I know she will help. I met her and she's not like the others in Perfect. She's different. She's like one of us just living in there."

"Violet's right," Boy said looking up, "she took me in sometimes, when the Watchers were chasing me. She can see us."

"No," William said angrily, "I won't have it. Leave her out of this, I can't lose her twice."

As William walked away a little girl of about six stood up from the sea of seated orphans, her jar of yellowish gas held aloft.

"Em...If you're going to your old house Mr. Archer can I come too?" she said nervously, "My house is on your street and I want to give this back to my Mammy. Boy said if she gets her imagination back she'll remember who I am."

Violet looked at the little girl then back at William Archer.

"Please William," she said, "I think I have a plan."

CHAPTER 31

The Reunion

After going vigorously through Violet's plan for anything that could go wrong, they waited until cover of darkness before slipping out through the gates of No Mans Land. They made their way towards the intersection that marked the entrance to Perfect. Boy moved ahead of the party to peer around the corner.

"There's about five Watchers at the bottom of the road," he whispered.

"Right," William said, addressing three orphans about Violet's age, "Distract them so we can get up this street. Nothing dangerous though please."

One of the orphans winked and the three scruffy scoundrels slipped round the corner of the street and marched laughing and joking towards the small band of Watchers. Once the Watchers were distracted, Violet, Boy and two more orphans each holding a jar of imagination, slipped round the corner and down the street in the opposite direction. They were followed slowly by Merrill and William carrying the "Reimaginator". At the top of the street they turned left onto a side alley that ran parallel to Perfect.

Soon they came to the house. Even in the darkness it was easy to tell William was nervous. Leaving down the machine, he turned his back on the group and walked to the door. His hand shook as he raised it to knock on the painted wood. Violet's stomach swam in butterflies. The click of the latch was magnified in the quiet of the street. A trickle of light fell out onto the cobble locked road. Then William Archer's face was illuminated by the opened door. His tense stance softened in the swiftness of his mother's embrace. Violet knew then that no matter what, her mother would never forget her.

Iris Archer held her son for what seemed like an eternity at the front door of her home. The others watched the roads nervously hoping the Watchers would not patrol by.

> "Mam," William said, eventually stepping back from her hold, "we need your help!"

> "Oh I knew something was brewing William," Iris Archer smiled, inviting in her ragged guests.

Surprisingly she greeted all by name. Maybe Iris wasn't as mad as everyone said.

"I knew you'd do something Violet," Iris said pouring her a cup of boiling water, "I saw it in your eyes, you have a touch of mischief about you."

Violet smiled, taking the comment as a compliment.

"I want to thank all of you," the old woman said grabbing her son's hand, "for bringing William back to me."

"I'm so sorry Mam," William said still shaken, "I should have come to see you but I couldn't..."

"I know," Iris said softly.

The room fell into a somber silence.

"I knew you'd come back," she spoke again after a while, "you have the fight. A spirit can be dulled but it never fully dies."

"They have Macula," William said, "I thought she was dead. Then I thought I was dead. I couldn't bear to try and be happy again so I gave up the fight. I'm so sorry Mam I should have come to you. I just thought it'd be better for you if I stayed away."

"It's okay William, you're back now. That's all that matters."

Iris took a sip from her cup and looked out past the faces gathered at her table into a place only she could go. A few moments later she spoke.

> "So they took Macula as well, I wondered about that? They robbed my life from me- those terrible two. I saw a little of it in them when they were young, they took after their father but who can predict this of their sons?"

She looked down at her hands clasped tightly round the mug.

> "It's my fault William. Georgie and Edward are all my fault."

> "We can stop them Mam. That's why we're here. We can change Perfect, we can take back our town," William said standing up to pull the blanket from the Reimaginator, "George and Edward have been robbing imaginations Mam. This will give them back."

Iris stood up and walked slowly around the machine. She asked questions of her son, questions impossible to understand, it was easy to see where the Archers got their brains.

> "I used to think she was a bit loony," Violet whispered across to Boy.

> "You get away with a lot when people think you're mad Violet," Iris smiled.

Boy laughed as Violet blushed. After Iris had inspected the machine and asked a few more questions of her son, they began to fill her in on their plans.

"We have Billy Bobbin's and Madeleine Nunn's imaginations here," Boy said, passing the jars over to Iris to inspect them, "we think they live on this street."

"I live two doors up. Well I mean my Mam does...I used too..." one of the orphans said stepping forward.

"I remember you pet," Iris replied, taking the little girl onto her knee, "Anna Nunn, I think they took you about a year ago?"

The girl nodded and began to cry.

"We think their families will be able to see them now," Violet interrupted, "we put William's potion into the tea so nobody in Perfect should be blind anymore. They won't fully recognise No Mans Landers though until we give them back their imaginations."

"Then Mam will know me; you promised," Anna said, looking straight at Boy.

"We want you to bring Madeleine and Billy here," William said to Iris, "once we get them here we can zap them with the Reimaginator. They'll recognise their children then, they'll believe us and..."

"Join the revolution," Iris smiled.

"Exactly," William replied, "then we'll get them to get others and slowly we'll build an army."

"I'll try my best," Iris said, "but I'm considered mad around here. I haven't spoken to either of them in as long as I can remember and I can't see how they'll follow me."

"Tell them that Edward and George want to meet them," Boy said suddenly, "I bet they'll come here for that, everybody loves them."

"I'm really not sure they'll believe me Boy."

"They believe anything you tell them in Perfect."

"You have a point," Iris laughed lifting the little girl from her knee and walking towards the door, "No time like the present. Well take your positions. I'll be back in a jiffy."

There was a sudden scramble from seats. William and Merrill lifted the Reimaginator so it sat center in the room. Boy and Violet took the jars off the table and gently lifting the lids, eased the contents into the glass box in the middle of William's machine. The imaginations floated through the space mixing together.

> "Won't they get mixed up?" Violet asked, pulling on William's shirtsleeve.

> "No Violet," William smiled, pointing at the glass, "Look. No two people think alike."

The imaginations had now settled one on top of the other, like oil and water.

Suddenly there were voices in the street outside.

> "Really they want to speak to us?" a man said, obviously delighted.

> "I knew Edward loved my Victoria sponge at the children's cake sale. I saw it on his face. He won't mind me calling him Edward will he, now that we're friends?"

> "No of course not Madeleine," Iris replied.

> "How is my hair Billy?" Madeleine asked, as Iris turned the key in the lock.

> "Perfect Madeleine," Billy replied, following behind the pruned woman into the house, "oh you have guests Iris."

> "Oh yes...they are..."

"Daddy..." one of the orphans cried. running towards Billy.

Boy quickly grabbed his shirt pulling him back and held tightly to the struggling seven year old.

"We're em...Iris's cousins," William said, quickly covering the scene.

"Oh how nice," Madeline replied, eyeing the struggle, "where are you visiting from?"

"Timbuktu," Violet piped up.

"Oh I've heard it's lovely," Billy smiled.

"Would anyone like tea?" Iris asked, pushing the kettle button.

"Oh I'd love some Iris," Madeleine replied, "Ours just isn't tasting the same lately.

Boy winked at Violet.

"So where are the twins?" Billy asked, breaking an awkward silence.

"Oh they...em they're upstairs. They'll be down in a minute," William responded. "While we wait, would you mind terribly if we took a family portrait? It's for our holiday snaps, the kids are growing up so quickly."

"Of course," Madeline replied, "I know what that's like. My oldest is almost seven."

"No I'm not I'm eight," Anna sniffled in the corner.

"Oh you're just a little older than mine then," Madeleine smiled.

"Okay, Billy you sit here and Madeleine you here," William said, placing the chairs just in front of the Reimaginator.

"But we're not part of your family?" Billy replied.

"Oh you are, we're all cousins," Violet smiled.

"But I've never been to Timbuktu," Madeline said taking a seat in front of the machine.

"Yes you have," Violet continued, "don't you remember, we went for a swim with the turtles and you said you thought they were lovely and then we went for a drive on the beach and we saw this giant elephant and he..."

Boy gave Violet a look that stopped her sudden rant.

"Oh maybe I do remember..." Madeleine said, looking curiously at Violet, "the turtles were lovely... I think. I do love turtles."

"So do I," Violet smiled, "See, we are cousins."

"That's a funny looking camera," Billy said.

"It's the latest thing," Boy replied, "Everyone has them in Timbuktu!"

"Right," William said, loudly bringing silence to the room, "Everybody say cheese."

He pulled the cord on the Reimaginator and the machine sprang to life. Each of the lungs on the side, the bits that looked like bagpipes, moved in and out, inflating and deflating at huge speeds. Suddenly the two imaginations were sucked up into separate pipes leaving the glass centre empty. The machine pulled in it's sides and, with an almighty noise like a huge sneeze, it spat out the imaginations. The greenish one flew for Billy Bobbins and the brownish one for Madeleine Nunn. The pair sat frozen. Their faces registered terror, as the separate strains of gas flew up their nostrils.

Immediately, their eyes shut and their heads fell forward. Billy slipped right down onto the floor while Madeleine slumped to the side resting against the table. Though the pair looked dead, William remained calm, a huge smile rested firmly on his face. Suddenly, each body started to rattle and before anyone knew what was happening they began to snore. It was louder than Violet's Dad and he had the loudest snore ever.

"What's happening?" Violet asked William.

"They're just re-adjusting. The imagination is at its strongest when we're asleep. That's why dreams are so real. They need to be asleep so they can reboot. It's a wondrous thing: the human body."

As quickly as the snoring had started it stopped and both Billy and Madeleine slowly opened their eyes.

"Where am I?" Madeleine asked sitting upright, "What happened?"

"Mam," Anna said jumping from her seat and running to her mother's side.

"Anna?" Anna is that you?" Madeleine cried, wrapping the little girl up in her arms, "I thought, I thought...I don't know what I thought..."

Billy's son threw himself onto his father's groggy body and both cried as they embraced.

After a while William helped Billy from the floor and everyone came together round the kitchen table. Both Madeleine and Billy had a world of questions. Their anger was obvious and they didn't take much convincing to agree to the plan.

As the sun was coming up over the town both Billy and

Madeleine left the house. They headed for Perfect to round up four specific friends. Boy and Violet left too but they headed for No Mans Land where they were to pick up four more orphans and their jars of imagination.

CHAPTER 32

The Give Away

It was another gloriously sunny day in Perfect. The Watchers were relaxed as, except for a handful of disruptive youngsters, not a soul from No Mans Land tried to enter the town. The Archers were happy too; the tills were overflowing as an unusual amount of customers looked to have their glasses repaired.

"People are getting very clumsy lately," George Archer remarked, fixing yet another cracked lens "must have a word to the Watchers. We don't want to mush people's brains altogether."

Their customers were unusually chatty that day and, distracted by small talk, the brothers didn't venture into their storeroom at all. Had they managed a trip they would have been shocked by the shelves that now hung bare. Regular trips led by either Boy or Violet meant that all imaginations now rested under the stairs of Iris Archer's hovelled home. By six that evening as Edward and George literally pushed their last customer out the door, a crowd had gathered in Iris's. A crowd that was about to change the face of Perfect forever.

"Who do I get next?" Madeleine Nunn, asked walking back to the door.

"These ones," Boy said, handing her a list of seven names he'd just taken from the top of the jars.

"I'm not sure Boy. Seven is a lot. I don't want to cause suspicion."

"You won't," William replied, pouring more jars into the Reimaginator, "We have to change as many people as quickly as possible, before my brothers discover the empty storeroom. The Reimaginator can take seven at a time, so I think that's what we should do."

"Ok, if you're sure," Madeleine said nervously exiting the house.

A few minutes gone by and Violet was stacking jars under Iris's table when Madeleine sprinted back past the window.

"I em...I was nearly caught," she cried, bursting in through the door to the tightly packed house, "I'm so sorry I forgot the rules. I nodded at the Watchers."

"You what?" William said, standing up from his seat.

"I'm so sorry William. I was nervous about bringing that many people back. I completely forgot I wasn't meant to see them!"

"Slow down Madeleine, what exactly happened?" William asked, pulling out a chair for her.

"Well I was walking into Perfect just passed the group of Watchers. They were playing cards you see..."

"And," William said, trying to speed up the story.

"And well, I was just minding my own business when one of them looked up at me. I caught his eye and trying to hide my nerves, I nodded. I don't know why I did it. I'm so sorry."

"Did he say anything?" Violet asked, from her spot on the floor.

"Well at first nothing. I didn't even realize I'd done it. Then he shouted after me and I stopped and asked him what the matter was,"

"No!" Violet cried, "you're not supposed to be able to see them!"

"I know that Violet!" Madeleine snapped, "I think I covered it up though. I said I used to be in Perfect but was thrown into No Mans Land a few days ago."

"Did they believe you?" Boy asked.

"Well..."

Madeleine was just about to answer when a loud knock hammered the door. Every soul in the room stopped breathing. Iris Archer immediately shot up from the table beckoning everyone to grab an imagination.

"Quickly take them into the garden and out through the fence Boy," she said, "you know the way. Go now. Hurry!"

Boy nodded and quickly directed everyone out of the house. Violet, William and Merrill moved the Reimaginator into the back room and watched the proceedings through a gap in the door.

"You see Iris me dear, she was still wearin her glasses. Now why would someone from No Mans Land be needin to wear their glasses?" the Watcher smiled, as he barged past Iris into the house, followed by a gang of his bandits.

"I don't know what you mean, who's she?" Iris asked, "It's just me here, me on my own, on my ownie, ownie, own. Like always. Just the walls to talk to here. You want tea? I like visitors; I haven't had anyone to talk to in as long as memory serves me."

"Come on now and don't play the fool Iris Archer," the Watcher growled, pushing her frail body up against the white washed wall, "we all know you're not as stupid as you look. I'm not neithers!"

"I'm not stupid?" Iris smiled.

"Lads search the house," the Watcher said, pushing the old woman down into a wonky chair.

"We knows something's up and you're gonna tell us what it is," the Watcher roared, as William pushed Violet out a back window into the garden.

Quickly she sprinted across the grass and clambered through a hole in the fence. The others stood waited in an alleyway behind the house.

"What's going to happen to Iris?" Violet asked breathlessly.

"She'll be fine Violet," William said, "they won't hurt Mam. No matter what they think of me I know my brothers wouldn't harm her."

"What about our plan?" Boy whispered.

"We need a new one," Violet said, before William could respond.

CHAPTER 33

Let The Battle Begin

Darkness had fallen once more as Violet and Boy snuck along a deserted side road into Perfect. Violet tiptoed up to the corner ahead and peered around. A huge crowd of Watchers congregated in the main square having abandoned their posts. There were lots of them, millions even.

They were gathered round a park bench that sat centre in a pristine flowerbed. Sitting on the bench, her face stern and body stiff was Iris Archer. Edward and George were perched either side of their mother.

"What are they doing?" Violet whispered.

"Waiting for us," Boy replied, "we have to tell William."

The pair sprinted back up the street as quietly as possible and didn't stop until they reached the entrance to No Mans Land. William Archer stood just inside the gates, his back to the Reimaginator, his front to an elated crowd. Everyone was hugging and there were lots of tears.

The people of Perfect, the ones that had been changed, were reunited with lost friends and family. The streets of No Mans Land were alive with talk of revolution. People who once rubbished William now brandished all sorts of tools ready to invade Perfect.

"It's happening," William smiled, hugging the pair as they reached his side, "it's really happening, we'll take Perfect tonight..."

"They're onto us, they're already waiting in the square. They have Iris," Boy interrupted, pushing back from William's embrace.

"How many of them?" the older man asked, his tone suddenly serious.

"Lots," Violet replied, "more than us by a long way. I didn't know they had so many Watchers!"

"I don't know if we can beat them," Boy continued, "we haven't changed enough people yet."

"We can change more," Violet said quickly, "I know we can."

"How Violet?" William asked, "they know we're coming now. They know something's up."

"What if we distract them?" Violet replied.

William Archer and his makeshift army strode through the gates of No Mans Land towards Perfect. William didn't look at the ground as he had in the past, he was soldier straight and focused.

Boy and Violet watched the huge group leave then quickly moved along the side roads towards the opposite end of the town followed by the orphans. They carried with them the remaining imaginations and William Archer's machine. Slotting into place at the other end of the square, the Watchers, distracted by Williams approach, didn't notice them.

> "William it's been a long time," Edward shouted, addressing his brother from his place on the bench.

> "I'm sure you've missed me Edward," William smiled.

All eyes were on the brothers face off. Not a soul paid heed to the small band of children who fiddled with a strange machine and jars of coloured gas at the other end of the square. Hurriedly, Violet poured seven more imaginations.

> "Of course. You're my favourite brother. I hope I've told you that before," Edward continued.

> "Eh, I thought I was..."

"George," Edward snapped, silencing his taller twin, "anyway we are impressed, somewhat, with your little rebellion William, but it's time to call a halt. You don't want anything to happen to poor old mother do you?"

"Old!" Iris spat, "Edward Archer, I could give you a seeing to when you were a boy and I can still do it now!"

Edward reddened round the ears.

"You have Macula!" William shouted, louder than necessary.

Edward looked at George who shrugged.

"Yes I know about her Edward and all this time you made me believe she was dead."

The crowd behind William hissed and shouted, swelling forwards towards the Watchers. Alerted by the noise, the people of Perfect began to open their doors. The plan was working.

"Oh perfect, we have an audience," William smiled, looking around.

As the brothers continued their banter, Boy with the help of some orphans lifted the Reimaginator. Madeleine had given Violet all the information she needed, so she knew who lived in every home. Silently she beckoned Boy over to a man standing perplexed on his doorstep.

"Billy Doyle," she whispered.

Boy pressed the button and a shot of purple gas flew from the machine up the unsuspecting man's nose. Just like the others he fell to the ground asleep. Violet pointed at another man and the scene repeated. Soon people were falling asleep all over the street. Quickly they filled and refilled the Reimaginator. They were making their way slowly through the street when a lady spotted the group. Eyeing the sea of unconscious bodies she let out a bloody scream.

"They're killing us, they're killing us!" she roared.

Violet froze. All eyes, Edward and George Archer included, turned towards them.

"What!" Edward roared furiously, spying his sleeping flock.

"Attack!" William Archer shouted, seizing upon the confusion.

Following his lead, the army of No Mans Landers raced screaming towards the stunned and silent Watchers. The crowd of tool wielding, ragged people charged towards their captors, the years of exile etched on their faces. Anger burned through their eyes.

"Violet, Violet. Come on. We still have a job to do!" Boy roared, shaking his frozen friend.

Her body woke. The streets were manic as Watchers were sparring against locals and once sleeping Perfectionists rose from their slumber to join the fight. The unchanged were not hard to spot standing still amidst the chaos. Violet ran straight for a woman just metres away.

"Sinead Cribits," she roared, pointing at the lady.

"I have her, I have her," one of the orphans shouted running forward to fill the Reimaginator with murky gas.

Within seconds Boy pushed the button and Sinead was unconscious. Violet fought her way through the sea of battling bodies to point at another Perfectionist. The jars of imagination were dwindling. Their plan was working. More and more waking bodies pulled themselves up from the ground to join the No Mans Landers.

Violet was pointing at another stunned onlooker when Boy roared and his body collapsed to the ground. George Archer loomed large above him.

"Think you'll take Perfect?" he smiled, a golf club hung loosely by his side, "not without this machine you won't!"

The tall twin took a swing at the Reimaginator. Glass flew through the air in all directions. Boy crawled away helpless as William Archer's machine was smashed to smithereens.

"And you, you've been the bane of this place from the beginning," George Archer spat.

He raised the golf club above his head and strode towards Boy. Violet's friend had just fumbled up onto his feet when George Archer brought the club down on his back once more.

"No," Violet roared, running blindly for the giant.

Anger pulsed through her veins; she bared her teeth and bit deep into George Archer's hand. The taller twin screamed dropping his weapon.

"You nasty pest!"

He grabbed Violet by the hair and pulled her close enough to smell his stinking breath.

"I'm gonna make you watch while I pulverize your friend."

Violet squirmed in his grasp as George Archer bent to pick up his club.

> "Who knew playing golf would come in so useful? I have a great swing, everyone in the club says so," he smiled, dragging Violet over to where Boy lay, "I often wonder: if a golf ball could, would it scream when I hit it?"

Violet cried out as the club crashed towards Boy's head. Suddenly she was shunted sideways and hit the ground with a painful thud. There was a struggle beside her. Quickly she crawled away to where Boy laboured onto his knees.

> "What happened?" Boy asked, "I thought he'd kill me. I thought I was dead."

> "It's William," Violet gasped, "he saved you. He saved us."

William Archer wrestled his older brother on the ground just metres away. Violet pulled her friend off the road to the relative safety of the footpath. For a moment they rested gathering their breath amongst the madness.

The fight was in full flow. The people of Perfect and No Mans Land fought side by side against the Watchers. They were winning the battle. Woken up to their new reality, adults and orphans fought like warriors.

"Violet," Boy said, dragging her attention away, "Look!"

Edward Archer stood solemn at the other side of the square. The stocky man watched in horror as his dreams crashed down around him. Suddenly, his gaze fell on William and George exchanging blows. His face changed. With swift and purposeful movement, he disappeared down a side street.

"He's up to something," Boy said, rising gingerly to his feet, "we have to follow him."

CHAPTER 34

Choices

Boy spoke with certainty, and though Violet didn't want him to be, he was right. They had to split up.

"We don't know what direction he's gone Violet," Boy said, speaking quickly, "it's either the shop or the Ghost Estate. I'll go to the shop if he's not there I'll meet you in the estate, okay?"

Violet nodded though chasing after Edward Archer alone wasn't on her list of favourite things.

"I know you're scared but we have to do this. It's for them," Boy said, pointing to the mayhem, "and for William and for your parents. You want them to be safe; you want them back don't you?"

"Of course," Violet snapped.

"Well then come on," he said, pulling her onto her feet, "Go through No Mans Land. Just find out what he's up to. Whatever you do don't approach him. He's probably gone to the shop anyway so you won't have to worry about meeting him."

"And what about you? What if you meet him?"

"I'll be fine," Boy smiled.

Violet waited as her friend crossed the square ahead of her. She was just dodging the fist of a Watcher when Boy turned and called her name.

"Violet. Be safe okay?"

She could manage was a nod, anything else would break her voice and she wasn't crying in front of Boy. Shaking off her nerves, Violet turned on the spot and raced towards No Mans Land. Guilt ate her up as she ran through the deserted streets. She didn't wish Boy luck or safety. What if something happened to him? He was her best friend.

Suddenly there was movement ahead. She stopped. A short, stout figure passed through the barbed wire gates into No Mans Land. Edward Archer. It was too late to run back and get Boy. It was up to her now. She had to follow him.

No Mans Land was empty. The streets were a mess, as if every soul suddenly dropped what they were doing to evacuate the town. Like a warm seat when someone's just left.

Edward Archer moved as fast as his fat figure could through the claustrophobic alleyways, coming to a halt in the middle of a particularly dingy street. Although all of No Mans Land was in disrepair this place had to be one of the worst. Every window on every home was broken and rubbish piled knee deep along the edges of the street. A rat scampered over Violet's foot stopping to nibble on her big toe nail. Horrified, she kicked the creature away.

Holding her nose, she crouched down behind a bin of rotting nappies as Edward Archer disappeared inside one of the derelict buildings. Flies that had been enjoying a feast of moldy baby poo now swarmed round her face. A skull and crossbones and the words "The Everything Evil Shop" were graffitied on the battered iron door William disappeared behind. Torn and tattered posters patterned the shop front with headlines like *Passion for Poison?* or *Mad about Murder?* Violet's heart pounded. What could Edward Archer want from a place like this?

A few minutes later, the door screeched round it's hinges and Edward Archer returned to the street. He was carrying a small, slim object barely visible through the barrage of flies.

"Oh you pretty Pistol," he smiled, stroking the long black neck of the deadly metal.

Violet panicked. Edward Archer had a gun! She lost her balance against the bin causing it to rattle. Edward swiftly shoved his purchase into his pocket and looked around the empty street. Violet ducked further down and waited. Droplets of sweat ran down her forehead.

His suspicions taken by a rat running out from behind some bins, Edward continued his journey. Violet followed a safe distance behind as he passed back through the alleyways and out into the main square of No Mans Land. He then took off in the direction of the Ghost Estate.

How was she going to stop him? He had a gun! What was he doing with a gun? Suddenly something caught her eye. A swish of material. A flower pattern forgotten until now. She stopped dead and turned. Rose Brown stood in the middle of the empty road. The base of her flowery skirt swung round her ankles. She moved nervously from foot to foot.

"Mam," Violet whispered, her voice trembling.

Rose didn't answer.

"Mam," Violet said, running to her mother side, "Mam, what are you doing here?"

"Oh I'm sorry. Were you speaking to me young girl? I thought you were addressing your mother. I suppose

I am the only one in this strange little place," Rose Brown replied, looking sheepishly around.

"Mam! Mam please, it's me," Violet choked, her voice breaking.

"I'm sorry, I think you're a little confused."

"You can't have forgotten me already. You can't Mam. Please! I only left a few days ago."

Her mother eased away from Violet.

"I don't know how I ended up in this place," she stuttered, turning her back on her daughter, "I was walking towards town and I saw those pillars. I'd never noticed them before. Isn't that odd? They are quiet huge..."

"It's No Mans Land Mam. It's where I've been. I've missed you so much..."

"Please little girl," Rose interrupted, "I'm not comfortable with you calling me your mother. Have you hit your head dear? Maybe it's this place. It is very confusing. Come on I'll bring you back to Perfect and help you find your parents."

Violet searched her mother's face for some recognition,

something that told her the last ten years had not been forgotten. Rose moved further backwards away from her daughter.

"Do you happen to know how to get out of here? I have to get to the shop; ran out of eggs you see. You can't make Madeira cake without eggs," she laughed nervously.

"I'll get William," Violet said suddenly, "That's what I'll do. I'll get William. He'll fix the Reimaginator and then he'll fix you. I have your imagination Mam. I left it in Iris's."

"I think you've banged your head dear. Anyway it was lovely to meet you but I must be on my way."

"I can help you get out of here," Violet shouted, quickly incase her mother ran away, "Please, please, follow me."

Her mother looked around cautiously and after a little hesitation followed her daughter. They were just passing through the square when a loud bang shook the streets. Violet and Rose jumped in unison.

"My goodness that sounded like a gun shot!" Rose gasped, her hands cupping her mouth.

It had to be Edward! Boy, her Dad, Macula, William, Violet was about to abandon them all. Finding her mother had pushed them from her mind.

"Mam," she said, quickly changing her tone, "you have to stay here. There's trouble in Perfect. I have to go but I'll be back for you. I promise."

"I'm not your mother little girl. Please stop calling me that!"

"I'm sorry, I'm sorry," Violet stuttered, thinking on her feet, "its em...it's the Archers. They asked me to find you. They said you make the best...em...the best Madeira cake in Perfect. They want you to make some for a party they're having..."

"A party, how wonderful. Why didn't you say so sooner little girl. We must get going then. I really need those eggs now," Rose said, walking towards the gates.

"No!" Violet shouted, "No they said to wait here. They are getting the eggs delivered here. The shop is closed for Christmas."

"Closed for Christmas but it's only September?"

"Oh Christmas is early this year," Violet said, pulling

over an abandoned crate, "Sit here and don't move until I come back. The Archers are very excited."

"Okay but make sure and hurry back with the eggs won't you?"

Violet nodded then sprinted down the road Edward Archer had taken just a short time earlier. She passed through the streets at bullet speed and without hesitation ran headlong into the Ghost Estate. The place was still glacier cold but the sadness didn't affect her. Her heart and soul were on fire. She was going to save her family.

CHAPTER 35

Edwards Escape

A little into the estate Violet slowed her pace. Edward Archer was about. She was nearing Macula's house when another shot ripped the air. Suddenly the place was filled with the cry of a thousand screeching babies. The eye plants had woken. Goose pimples dimpled her skin.

Just then two figures emerged from the fog ahead walking through the park in her direction. She ducked down by one of the half built walls.

Edward Archer pushed Eugene Brown roughly across the grass. Her father's weakened body stumbled on several occasions as he tried to keep up with the twin's brisk pace. Her usually strong father was now feeble. She turned away, plunged her fingers deep into the loose earth and gripped the soggy soil. Her body shook with the pressure of an inner scream. From Boy she'd learned the art of timing. If she acted now any chance would be lost.

"Faster Eugene!" Edward Archer roared, "We have to

get out of here. That blasted brother never could keep to his own business."

"I can't move any faster," Eugene Brown coughed, tripping over a tuft of grass, "I need food."

"I fed you last week! Now move it or it's your eyes I'll be stealing next."

"Where are you taking me?"

"Somewhere else; I'll create my own Perfect where William won't find me."

"What about my family? You promised they'd be okay."

"Oh they are Eugene. Well your wife is at least. She's perfect. As for that daughter of yours, I left her in the middle of a battle with any luck a Watchers squashed her."

"Violet's fighting back? I knew it. She's braver than all of us."

Her father's voice was weak. He was standing on Macula's lawn just metres away, a broken man. She had to do something. Suddenly Violet was on her feet.

"I'm here! I'm here Dad!"

Eugene Brown turned to face his daughter. All weakness left him and he ran. Wrapping her in his arms he held Violet tighter than ever before. All her bravery fled and she collapsed into him, a kid again.

Another shot cut the night. Eugene shoved Violet behind his back and turned to face Edward. The stocky twin pointed his pistol at the pair. His cocked arm shook as he stared in hatred.

"Eugene. GET.BACK.HERE!"

"You've had your day Edward Archer. I won't let you take my family from me," her father's voice was strong and steady like it used to be.

"I don't want your stinking family, they can go to hell as far as I care. I only need you!"

Edward's eyes bulged from their sockets.

"You can't have me. You've taken enough."

"I can have whatever I want. I have a whole town at my finger tips."

"Had," Violet shouted, sneaking out from behind her father, "the town is not yours anymore. William saved it!"

Something moved in the upstairs window of the house. A shadow passed by the pane, rested for a moment then pulled back into the room. It was Macula Archer.

"William is better than you'll ever be," Violet roared, drawing all attention towards her.

"Oh William, William, William, the prodigal son. Everybody loves William. Well he can take Perfect if he wants but I have Macula!" Edward laughed.

"You kept her prisoner," Violet shouted, loud enough for Macula to hear, "You told her lies, made her believe William was dead when he's not!"

"You better learn to shut your mouth little girl!" Edward's voice was full of venom.

Macula silently prized open the window. Eugene had seen her now too.

"Just go Edward, we won't try to stop you. Perfect is gone. The game's over," he said.

"Not without Macula!"

"She doesn't love you!" Violet roared.

"I will not leave without Macula! William took my

mother from me, but who wants that old bat anyway! He took my friends too, they were a bunch of brainless buffoons - but then he took her and she was meant to be mine! I loved her. I still love her and you Browns are not going to stop us being together!"

Edward Archer charged for the house. The window was fully open. It was now or never. Violet raced across the lawn after him.

"She doesn't love you, she loves William!" she roared.

The stout twin stopped and turned. His eyes changed. Hatred was replaced by evil. She'd made a mistake. Time slowed. He cocked the gun. A faint click. BANG!

Suddenly time resumed. Violet was catapulted backwards. The air left her lungs as she smashed against the soil. Everything went hazy, foggy. She couldn't see. Slowly shadows merged. Her father's face floated in the sky above.

"Violet! Violet are you okay?"

"I'm...em..." she couldn't reply.

The weight. Something was sitting on her chest. Edward must have shot her. It always happened that way in films. The person took an age to realize they'd been hurt. There was no pain. There was never any pain in the movies.

"That boy. He saved your life!" her father stammered.

"What?" Violet said bolting upright.

Boy lay unconscious on the grass beside her. His body floppy just as it'd been when he'd fought the Watcher. Quickly Violet crawled to his side.

"Boy, Boy please wake up," she cried.

Her father pulled her aside to examine him.

"Will he be okay Dad?" she sobbed, "he's my best friend."

The house door opened and Macula Archer ran out across the lawn.

"Will he be okay?" she panted, reaching Boy's side. "He saved your life."

Violet was hysterical as Macula pulled her into her arms and away from the scene. She was shaking. Pain, like nothing before, dug into her chest. A hole was scooped from her stomach where Boy, her best friend, had been. She couldn't lose him. Not now. Not after everything.

Edward Archer was sprawled flat across the lawn behind Macula. The thickest book ever lay open beside him.

The Worlds One Thousand Worst Eye Ailments.

"I dropped it on his head," Macula smiled, hugging Violet closer.

Boy's lips were a faint blue now. His cheeks pale too. The hole in her stomach grew larger. Edward Archer wouldn't get away with this. She broke from Macula's arms and turned towards the unconscious twin. He was gone.

Quickly she scanned the area. His stocky figure stumbled along the estate road towards the graveyard. Furious, she sprinted after him. Her blood boiled propelling her legs forward. Everything was his fault and now he'd killed her best friend, her only friend. Edward Archer had to suffer. He had to pay.

He staggered under the hazy street lamp and slipped through the turnstile into the graveyard. Violet followed. She wasn't afraid. She was angry. She couldn't let him get away with what he had done. The putrid smell of disintegrating bodies grabbed her nostrils. She was standing on the path that divided the cemetery. Gravestones hovered either side. She ducked down behind a mossy one and waited. He had to be here, somewhere. Her heart beat loudly and her breath formed icy clouds in front of her nose. The graveyard was dead still.

"I know you're in here Edward Archer," she shouted, trying to sound brave, "You won't get away with this. The whole of Perfect is on the way."

"You're on your own Violet, aren't you afraid?" the twins voice echoed.

There was a sudden movement. Quickly she turned. A figure passed behind her. She raced after him. He was quick, cutting swiftly through the tightly packed headstones. She tripped and fell. Her palms were bleeding. The person stopped to stare. Laughter wrapped the graveyard. The fog was too thick. She couldn't see a face, but the figure was too thin to be Edward Archer.

"What's wrong Violet?" the stranger laughed, moving towards her.

"Violet. Violet where are you?" her father's desperate voice cried from the graveyard wall.

"Looks like I'll have to introduce myself another time. Pass my regards onto Boy," the stranger sneered, then disappeared behind a tombstone.

Violet raced to the where the stranger had stood but they'd gone. Vanished, as if by magic. The tomb was covered in thick moss, which she scraped away to read the inscription. The text was too damaged by time to make sense. A tiny wooden cross rested against the bottom corner of the tombstone like an afterthought. Two broken branches held together with a single nail. Hanging from the cross was a hand written card covered in grimy plastic.

HERE MARKS THE FINAL RESTING PLACE OF A.W. ARCHER. MORE THAN HE DESERVES.

"Violet, what were you doing running off alone," her father snapped, reaching her side.

"I'm sorry Dad," she stammered looking up, "It's just I wanted to catch Edward Archer. He can't get away with what he did to Boy. He's gone Dad. I couldn't find him!"

"I know Violet," her father soothed, pulling her up into his arms, "but don't worry we'll track him down, those Archers are not as clever as they think. As for your friend Boy, he's going to be fine. It's just a bump to the head."

"Boy's alive?"

"And kicking," her father laughed, as Violet jumped around in his arms.

"Wohoo...Boy's alive!"

Happiness, relief and exhaustion flooded her body and, after celebrating, Violet buried her head deep into her Dad's shoulder and cried. Her tears were not for sadness or loss but for Boy. He was going to be okay.

"Dad," Violet asked, as Eugene Brown carried her across the Ghost Estate, "who's A.W. Archer?"

"I don't know Violet but if they're related to Edward and George I'd prefer not to!"

Macula was nursing Boy on the soggy grass when they reached them. Her father left Violet down on the lawn and picked up Boy, he was still too hazy to walk.

"Come on," Eugene smiled, heading towards the exit of the Ghost Estate, "lets go home."

There was a piece of paper on the lawn where Boy had lain. Violet picked it up. It must have slipped from his pocket in the fall.

So you'll never be invisible.

Now she knew what was familiar about the note, the handwriting, she'd seen it before. Holding the prized paper firm in her fist she ran to catch the others.

"I think this is yours," Violet said, tugging on Macula Archer's sleeve.

CHAPTER 36

Our Town

The whole town was already gathered in the square when Boy and Violet sprinted down the main street past the newly planted flowerbeds.

"I still think those eyes are creepy," Boy shuddered.

"Well you better get used to them they're all over town. Edward Archer will never sneak back in here with all of those watching out for him," Violet laughed, "Come on we're late. Mam is always giving out to me for delaying."

"I can't get used to this parents thing," Boy said, racing beside his friend, "I mean I never had to obey anyone before."

"You love it!" Violet teased, sprinting ahead.

Everyone was standing round a small red curtain when the pair arrived. William Archer's hand rested on the cord as he finished his speech.

"And now let us all forget our Perfect past and move onto our future," he smiled, pulling tight on the rope.

The curtains glided gracefully apart to reveal a marble etched plaque, *Welcome to Town* it read. The place erupted in applause.

"Town, what kind of a name is that?" Boy smirked.

"Well you can't talk," Violet laughed, "and anyway it's not just any town Boy. It's our Town."

THE END.

If you like Perfect, please review it on Amazon, I'd be extremely grateful and Boy and Violet would be delighted, you see they really want to be famous!

Helena Duggan is a writer and graphic designer living in Kilkenny, Ireland. If you have any questions about Boy or Violet or anything in the whole world, please contact her. She loves talking, never really shuts up actually!

These are her websites

Helddesign.ie (that's for all her design work)
Helenaduggan.com (that's for all her writing stuff)

A Place Called Perfect is available for sale on Amazon.com and other online outlets. It is also available as an eBook. Please check out helenaduggan.com for further details.

Helena is also on Facebook and Twitter, you'll find the links through her website. (She's not the best tweeter in the world, leaves that to the birds!)